Skull Mountain Bandit

SKULL
MOUNTAIN
BANDIT

Terrell L. Bowers

AVALON BOOKS
THOMAS BOUREGY AND COMPANY, INC.
NEW YORK

PRINTED IN THE UNITED STATES OF AMERICA
BY HADDON CRAFTSMEN, SCRANTON, PENNSYLVANIA

Skull Mountain Bandit

CHAPTER ONE

Guy Kolter leaned against the tall oak tree that stood in front of the Denver courthouse. He had no stomach for hangings, but it was his proper duty to witness the death of the man he'd brought to justice. There were many spectators in the crowd, a number who'd taken their children to see what could happen to someone who went against the law.

The trapdoor beneath Joe Boska, the condemned man, dropped with a bang, and then the noose around his neck choked the life out of him.

The crowd was noisy, for Joe Boska had killed six people—including two young girls—in a series of stagecoach robberies. Many people thought hanging was too good—too quick—for such a lowlife. Well, at least they were rid of him now.

Guy was among the first to walk away. He thought Boska deserved what he got, sure. But Guy also thought death was a terrible thing, even when it claimed a vicious gunman.

"Hey, Kolter!" a voice called as Guy started up the street.

Turning around, Guy recognized one of his fellow detectives. "What say, Hank? I didn't expect you back in town so soon."

"Turns out that my case was no murder but a suicide, after all," Hank Wilks said. "After a bit of footwork, I rounded up a doctor that was treating Jamison for acute tuberculosis. I figure the pain got to be too much for him."

"I guess you just saw the results of my investigation," Guy said.

"You get all the good ones," Hank chuckled. "If the police were organized, they'd have tracked Joe down after that first robbery and killing."

"Boska was a tough man to track down. But the father of those Mallory girls wanted him arrested for sure. I spent over a solid month on nothing but finding him. People talked to me who might not have spoken a word to any regular lawman."

"Besides which, the local badges don't get anything extra for their labors. I bet you made the agency some money on this caper. The Mallorys certainly are well off enough to pay handsomely."

"But all their money won't bring the girls back to life," Guy sighed.

"Guess not. Say, you been over to the office today?" Hank asked.

"No. I'm supposed to be on leave. Is something up?"

"The captain has another job lined up for you. I was interested in it, but I'm stuck with the armed guards that are protecting that gold shipment that's coming into Denver."

"Well, that's how it goes," Guy said.

"Yeah, you get all the real detective work. All I get mostly is armed-guard stuff. At least it seems that way," Hank said.

"Guess I'll wander over and see what the captain has in mind."

"How about some lunch first? I got paid this morning. I'll even pick up the bill."

"I doubt that you'll make that offer to me twice, Hank, but I haven't got any appetite right now."

"Sure, I understand," Hank said. "You always were a little squeamish about watching any killing. Even an outlaw's hanging."

"I'll be seeing you," Guy replied, turning to walk away. He didn't wait to see the faint smirk that was bound to appear on the other man's face.

Guy knew what Hank thought of him. Everyone working for the agency felt the same way: Guy Kolter was the best in his field at deducing facts, at sorting out clues, but he wasn't a man who would reach for his gun quickly.

It wasn't his muscles or eyes that moved too slowly. It was his brain that balked at killing another human being.

In two years with the detective agency, he'd only fired once. He'd wounded a suspect on that occasion, but Jeff Portt, one of his fellow detectives—his best friend—was killed. Many people believed that a quicker reaction by Guy would have saved his friend.

Guy had relived the moment in his mind a thousand times. He'd had nightmares about it, waking up in a guilty sweat afterward. He was reliving that moment now as he entered the small building where the Denver Detective & Armed Escort Agency had its office.

The owner and director of the agency was Captain George Benton. He'd been a Pinkerton detective toward the end of the Civil War, then branched out to start up his own service. Though he was basically an honest man, he'd given himself the unearned title of captain because it lent him authority.

Guy found the captain behind his desk, where he spent much of his time. These days Benton did little fieldwork, usually burying himself under a mountain of papers. He wore spectacles when he read or wrote, but he always removed them when a client entered.

"Come in, Kolter. I've been hoping you'd stop by."

"Hank said you wanted to see me, but I thought my leave started today. I'm supposed to get a week off—remember?"

"Sure, sure," Benton said with an amiable smile. "We'll get around to that."

Guy sat in the chair next to the captain's desk. He had his hat in his hands, so he toyed with it, waiting for his boss to spring the new job on him.

"Ever hear of Crystal Creek?"

"Can't say that I have."

"Well, it's over the San Juans, the other side of Silverton." The captain looked over his glasses. "You know about Silverton, don't you?"

"It was made a county seat some time back."

"That's right. The Crooke Smelter is going great guns there, and a lot of the small silver mines are shipping their ore to them for processing."

"What's the matter? Is someone high-grading on a mineowner?"

Benton shook his head and passed Guy a piece of paper.

Guy looked at the scribbled writing. "Somebody making a joke?"

"No. The letter came with a five-hundred-dollar fee. Don't find many clients willing to pay in advance—not that kind of money."

Guy again looked at the paper and read aloud. "'Enclosed is your fee. Find the man who killed Zack Lorring, and you'll get another five hundred dollars. Look for the killer in Crystal Creek, Colorado.'" He gave the note back to Benton.

"Pretty handsome offer. What do you make of it?" Guy asked.

"The writer is most likely a man, the paper is from a ledger of some kind, and the instrument used for writing is an ordinary quill. The words show some education, and our client has enough money to spend that he intends to hire the best."

"How'd the letter arrive?"

"It was simply mailed—money and all—straight from Silverton," the captain said.

"What kind of action do you want us to take?" Guy asked.

Benton took off his glasses and leaned back in his chair. He regarded Guy thoughtfully before speaking.

"You're still troubled by the death of your partner, aren't you?"

"There'll always be doubts about the way I handled that job, Captain. I underestimated how dangerous the suspect was. It turned out to be a fatal mistake."

"I've never killed unless it was the last resort, Kolter. Like you, I think it's better to reason with a man. Only, that particular fella was more dangerous than any of us thought. Well, I'd have likely hesitated before shooting him if I was in your boots. So don't be too hard on yourself. Hear?"

"Yes, sir."

"But don't make the same mistake again. There are times when you have to shoot fast. No two ways about it. Now I want you to take this assignment. It won't be easy. They only have a single sheriff covering a hundred miles around that way. If word gets out why you're there, you can expect this Zack Lorring's killer to try and get you."

"I get the distinct idea my leave has been canceled," Guy said.

"That's right. Strike while the iron is hot, I always say."

"Sometimes I wish I was a blacksmith. It could come in handy."

"I'll pick up some expense money for you and figure your time for this Joe Boska caper," Benton said. "You needn't pull out until tomorrow, unless you intend to go by stage."

"I prefer my own horse. So I'll start out tomorrow. Now I'll head over to the boardinghouse and get my gear packed."

Benton said, "Fine. Come back in two hours. I'll have your expense money and what I owe you for the last job. I know I can count on you to clear up this Lorring murder. You're a good man."

Guy hoped the captain was right.

CHAPTER TWO

The air was still brisk, for it was only May. The Colorado mountains were not in the habit of giving up their coolness quickly. Even at the lower elevations, it didn't begin to warm up until midmorning.

Guy had spent last night in the shelter of an abandoned cabin. The other nights he'd slept under the sky. He felt better, more rested, this morning, but his roan was worn down from the long trek over the rugged San Juan mountains. He hoped to reach Crystal Creek today and treat the sturdy mount to some grain and a couple days' rest.

He had not been riding long when he topped a knoll, where he could view the winding road below. It was the main route between Crystal

Creek and Silverton.

Looking down, Guy saw a man standing there, his hands high in the air. A second figure dressed completely in black—including a black hood that totally covered his head—pointed a gun at the first man, forcing him to remove his boots and hand them over.

As Guy put his horse into motion, the bandit in black got on a horse and led the other man's animal up a narrow ravine. The bootless man lowered his hands, then spied Guy coming toward him. He began shouting frantically, pointing toward the escaping bandit. Guy could only pick up something about the man's being robbed.

Bolting after the bandit, he saw the hooded man had turned the second horse loose. And now he was beating a hasty retreat up a winding, narrow path, which appeared to lead into a range of rocky buttes. Guy tried to keep after him. But it was hard going for a horse that had brought him over two hundred miles in five days.

Going around the brush, ducking tree branches, cutting through timber, Guy knew he couldn't overtake the bandit. Unless he happened to get knocked off his horse, the man would escape on the superior strength of his mount.

Guy urged more speed out of his jaded horse, hoping a final burst might panic the bandit and cause him to make a mistake. If he thought that Guy had a chance of overtaking him, he might slow down, get confused, do anything.

Rounding a bend in the trail, Guy suddenly had to rein his horse to a stop. For there on the ground, next to the path, was a woman. Her forehead was bruised, her riding skirt was mussed, and her hat lay a few feet away. She was unconscious or dead. Wandering through the brush, lost without any guidance, was the bandit's horse.

Guy pulled out his gun, sweeping the area, ready to fire instantly, half expecting a bullet to tear through him at any second.

There was nothing. Not a sound, other than a distant chirping bird.

Letting his horse blow, Guy climbed down from the saddle and walked over to the woman. He found her to be young—possibly twenty— with light-brown hair tangled about an attractive oval face. Even as he knelt next to her, she blinked her eyes open. Her hand went up to the bruise on her forehead.

"W-what happened? Who are you?"

"Easy, ma'am," Guy said, giving her a hand, helping her to sit up.

The woman gently rubbed the bruise on her

head. Then her brown eyes scanned his face with curiosity.

"You're not the man who hit me," she said. "He wanted my horse."

Guy looked at the steep incline ahead, the trail going nearly straight up in places. He shook his head. "He needed to steal a mountain goat. That's one tough escape route he took."

"He had a black hood over his face," she said. "He about ran me down, then demanded my horse. I tried to ride past him, but he struck me with the barrel of his gun. Now how am I supposed to ride out of here?"

Guy said, "I'll catch his horse. Maybe someone in town will recognize it. It could help to discover who that bandit is."

"I'm all right now," she said, a timid smile tracing her delicate lips, her eyes alive and sparkling. "Perhaps a bit dizzy, but I'm able to wait here alone, while you catch that other horse."

Guy returned to his own horse, took a last look at the young woman, then set out to capture the bandit's animal. As the horse was winded, it wasn't any chore to overtake him. Any hopes of identification were limited, for the animal was mustang stock. He had no brand and his markings were similar to those of a thousand wild horses from farther west. The saddle was a simple army saddle, like countless others. Even the reins were the dime-a-dozen style available at any livery stable.

Like a proper lady, the woman waited for Guy to give her a leg up to her horse. She seemed hesitant, sitting the horse like a man.

"I've never ridden astraddle before. I have an English saddle for ladies."

"Never could figure how you stayed in one of those in terrain like this."

She smiled again. "With good luck and strong fingernails."

"The name's Guy Kolter," he said. "I just rode in from Denver."

"Nicole Monday," she reciprocated. "I'm pleased to meet you, Mr. Kolter—even under such difficult circumstances."

"Speaking of which, I don't suppose you saw a man's boots?" he said.

"Boots?"

"That bandit robbed a man down there at the main trail. He even took his boots."

"All I really saw were stars dancing in front of my eyes," she replied. "Maybe the masked man threw them in the brush along the trail. It appears that he took his saddlebags—and mine."

"Did you have anything valuable in them?"

That smile again. "Only my soap and towel. There's a pond about another half mile from here. I was on my way to wash."

"You live around here?"

"I rented a small cottage at the base of Skull Mountain. There are two sheepherders who live near there as well. Not in my cabin, of course."

"Sheepherders and cattlemen have been at each other's throats for some time in Colorado. Aren't you afraid of getting mixed up in some kind of war?"

"There are no cattle in these hills. That's why the Quintons have their sheep here. They're nice young men, and it makes my living in the cabin more secure. The Utes are peaceful enough, but there are always renegades in any tribe. I like having someone near."

"It was no Indian that took your horse."

"I couldn't tell what he was, other than desperate," she said.

"He must have thought that I had a chance to catch him. He had no idea how tired my animal was."

"You said that it wasn't an Indian. How could you know that?" she asked.

"Utes are horse lovers. Natural riders. The bandit didn't ride like an Indian. He was too out of time with the horse."

"You're very observant, considering you didn't get close enough to shoot at him. That is, I figure you didn't. After all, I'd have heard any shots."

"You're right about that," he said.

"What brings you to Crystal Creek, Mr. Kolter?"

"Just looking up an old friend. He wandered this way some time back."

"It could be that I know him. Crystal Creek isn't very large."

"Name's Zack Lorring."

The girl looked thoughtful, a tight frown creasing her face. "You are a friend of Zack Lorring?"

"I knew him a bit during the war," Guy lied. "You know where I can find him?"

"In the Crystal Creek cemetary, I'm afraid. He was murdered a few weeks back."

Guy feinted surprise. "No? Really?"

She nodded. "They found him with a bullet in his back. His partner sold off their mine and took over the cafe in town. He swore to find out who had killed Zack, but that's the last I heard of anything being done."

"Then Zack had a partner, huh?" Guy said.

"Yes. Zack Lorring and Pack Johnson—Zack and Pack, as close as their names. Pack took Zack's death quite hard. I don't think I've even seen him smile since that day."

"Then you knew both men?"

"Their claim was next to that of Milo Gates, my fiance."

"You're engaged to a mineowner?"

She narrowed her eyes, a look of suspicion in them. "You ask an awful lot of questions for a stranger who's only passing through our valley."

"Can't help being nosy, Miss Monday," he said with a grin. "I've always had a curious nature."

"Well, don't be curious about Milo Gates and his affairs. He isn't a man who likes to be put upon or talked about. Just last month, a freighter slandered him while drinking at the Big Kitty Saloon. That freighter left town draped over his saddle, most of his teeth missing and his trousers full of cactus, courtesy of Ape Mongold and Taco Sanchez. Milo's men are loyal to him."

"I never heard of miners who didn't think that highgrading from the mineowner wasn't their special right, or that bad-mouthing the boss wasn't the favorite pastime."

"Not the men from the Gates Mine. You'll do well to remember that, whether you stick around for a few hours or a few days."

"Must comfort you, being engaged to such a powerful man."

The woman's cheeks and throat began to color noticeably, and her eyes grew cold. This was not the girl who enjoyed being teased.

"I think you'd better keep your visit with Pack very short. I don't think you have the kind of personality to get along in Crystal Creek."

He grinned, the action seeming to fuel the woman's anger. "Like I told you before, I'm kind of nosy. Guess that's why I went after that bandit. I can't seem to stay away from trouble."

"You butt heads with Milo Gates, and you'll never have to worry about trouble again. He'll bury you in Crystal Creek—next to your friend, Zack Lorring!"

As they talked, they had slowly retraced the tracks of the bandit. When they hit the main trail, they found the bootless man had recovered his own horse. He was starting in their direction as they came out of the trees. He obviously recognized the girl.

"Miss Monday?" he said, surprise written all over his face. "How did you get up here?"

"So you're the one to get robbed this time, Benny. I would have thought Milo would have

sent Flash or one of the other men with you.
Don't tell me you lost the payroll."

"That's just what happened," the man said
with a shake of his head. "Mr. Gates is going
to be real upset. You know that we've now lost
three payrolls in six weeks?"

"Someone is getting rich with your wages,
Benny. How do you like working for nothing?"

"I ain't working for nothing!" Benny showed
some backbone, although he didn't look very
formidable. "I got near two hundred dollars
coming to me, and I intend to collect! Mr. Gates
can't expect us to keep going without a dime.
Not one payday in six weeks!"

"This theft was your fault. Why didn't you
make a run for it and try to get away from
the bandit?" she said.

"Didn't even see him until he had a gun in
my face."

"You're supposed to be good with a gun. Next
to Flash Tokat, you're the fastest draw in
Crystal Creek."

"Being fast don't make no difference to a
scatter-gun, Miss Monday. That bandit had a
sawed-off 10-gauge Meteor double shotgun
pointed at me. You know what kind of hole
that would blow in a body?"

"I know what kind of a bruise it puts on
your head," she replied. "He used it to hit me."

She put a hand to her forehead. "It was enough to knock me off my horse. But I think the landing hurt more than his clout."

"You didn't see a pair of boots anywhere along the trail, did you?"

"Sorry, Benny. He must have taken them with him."

"I paid an awful lot for those. They were special embroidered in gold lace. I'll never be able to afford another pair like those."

"He won't dare wear them," Guy said. "If he sells them, a man could trace the boots back to him. Unless he's leaving the country, I can see no reason to steal boots he can't possibly use."

"I'll ride with you, Benny, to tell Milo," Nicole offered. "He won't be so mad if I'm there at the same time."

"He'll only wait to get me alone," Benny said sorrowfully. "I hate to think how mad he's going to be."

The three of them turned their horses toward town. Guy wondered just what kind of mess he was riding into. Could there be a connection between the bandit and the death of Zack Lorring? Would he find some answers, or would he be riding into a war of some kind?

CHAPTER THREE

Milo Gates lived in the biggest, grandest house in Crystal Creek. Not that he had much competition, as there were only a dozen shanty buildings, a few log cabins, and numerous tents and wagons around. One main street, rutted and muddied in a spot or two, went through the center of the settlement. One of the bigger places was the Big Kitty Saloon, and to the side, in a kind of lean-to, was Pack's Eatery.

"My business is across the street," Nicole told Guy, pointing to a little wooden shop. Only the word BAKERY was on the front window.

"You're not open today?" he asked.

"It's Sunday. I refuse to work on Sundays."

"I kind of lost track of days since I left Denver."

"What sort of work do you do, Mr. Kolter?"

"I make a career of sticking my nose into other people's business," he told her with a grin. "I'm kind of between jobs right now."

"Remember what I told you about Mr. Gates," she warned him. "He doesn't care for even idle curiosity."

"Maybe he's got something to hide," Guy ventured, watching the girl for her reaction.

She only put those soft brown eyes on him in a level gaze. "If he does, you wouldn't want to find it out. I told you that—"

"I know." He raised a hand to stop her. "I could end up in the Crystal Creek cemetery."

"Exactly."

They reined up in front of the mineowner's house, Guy quickly dismounting, then moving around to tie up the girl's horse. As luck would have it, he was just helping her down—his hands on her waist—as the door opened. He purposely let Nicole down to the ground next to him, not stepping away as quickly as would have been gentlemanly.

The girl noticed his actions, a flush of color rising instantly in her cheeks. Then she made the effort to move away from him, and he smiled at her.

The man on the porch wasn't smiling. He had hard eyes, a light blue in color, narrowed at Guy's actions. He regarded them both with a mild suspicion, but it was evident that he was even more concerned with Benny.

"Stone? Don't tell me you got robbed. I ain't in the mood to listen!"

"Even took my boots," Benny complained. "Honest, boss, I never seen him until he was right on me with a shotgun!"

The mineowner's square jaw grew rigid. He was quite a big man—maybe six feet, and a hundred and ninety pounds in weight—but he moved easily, jumping forward to open the gate on the small fence that surrounded his yard and house. It was then that he noticed the bruise on Nicole's forehead.

"Hey! You been hurt?"

She said, "Benny's bandit needed a fresh horse. He decided to take mine—over my objections."

"Filthy scum!" Milo roared. "We've got to put an end to that rotten, thieving sidewinder! I don't care what it costs. We've got to hire some trackers and hunt him down!"

"Eight hundred and seventy dollars," Benny said dejectedly. "I'm flat broke—and he even took my boots, too!"

"His damn robbing ain't doing me any good either, Stone. How can I pay you men when every cent is hijacked by some masked bandit?"

"What about the money you sent for? Won't it be coming on the stage?"

"If the stage gets through. This guy seems to be hitting every man that moves—'ceptin' maybe this jasper." Milo turned his attention on Guy, surveying him with cautious eyes. "What's your angle, Jack?"

"The name isn't Jack," Guy replied evenly, forcing a friendly smile to his face. "Fact is, I've never known a man with Jack as his first name."

"So why are you here in Crystal Creek?"

"Seems we fought a war to make men free a few years back. I reckon that gives me the right to visit your fair town, if I've a mind to."

"Mr. Kolter happened along right after the robbery," Nicole said, hurrying to enter into the conversation before the two got into a serious argument. "He might have caught up with him if the bandit hadn't taken my horse."

"Not Midnight?" Milo cried. "Not that beautiful animal I gave you for your birthday last week?"

"No. I was going to ride Midnight into town later. I was on one of the Quintons' mounts."

That brought a scowl to the man's face. "Why

do you have to associate with those sheepherders? I think you ought to move into town
and get away from them."

"They're very nice boys," Nicole said.

"They're sheepherders," he said distaste-
fully. "Everyone knows that men who run
sheep are strictly low-life."

"I've heard the same thing said of mine-
owners," Guy put in. "It just goes to show you
how different some people's viewpoints can be."

"You're a mouthy cuss, sonny. I don't cotton
to smart boys."

"I could tell that by your hired help," Guy
said, grinning. "A man with any brains
wouldn't have ridden the main trail—not
when he was carrying a payroll that was the
obvious target of a bandit."

"I only done what the boss told me to," Benny
cried. "You calling me stupid for following orders?"

"Not me," Guy said. "I only wonder at such
a great lack of precaution."

Milo took a step forward, his teeth bared,
fists clenched at his sides.

But Nicole was quick to react, stepping sub-
tly between him and Guy. "Milo thought that
Benny could pass the bandit's notice by the
simple act of being nonchalant. His ride

shouldn't have been suspect to the holdup man."

"Then this bandit either knows your plans, or he stops and robs every man who passes by. I'd say that your security is a little lax."

"Just what is your business, Kolter?" Milo demanded.

"You could say that I'm in the speculation business, Gates. I came to look over a mine or two, see what prospects there are for growth or business—that sort of thing."

"There ain't any mines for sale hereabouts, and you can tell by the size of the town that our growth has stopped. Why don't you mount up and keep riding?"

"Sounds like good advice," Guy replied, getting on his roan once more. He let his natural grin infuriate Gates. "However, I've just met a very pretty girl, my horse has worn his hooves down to his fetlocks, and I'm in need of a meal and some rest. I'll have to hold off leaving for a couple of days at least."

"Try and stay out of my way till you depart our fair town, Kolter. I don't like wiseacres, and I don't like you chasing after my woman."

Guy tipped his hat to Nicole. He thought she looked more concerned than the situation called for, but he didn't let it stop him from offering her his warmest smile.

"A real pleasure meeting you, Miss Monday. I certainly hope our paths cross again sometime—only under less unpleasant circumstances."

"Good day, Mr. Kolter."

"So long, Benny. Be careful that you don't do any thinking for yourself. That might be dangerous," Guy said.

"Yeah, thanks for nothing, Kolter."

Guy looked back at Milo Gates. The man seemed prepared to say something nasty, so he didn't offer him the chance. He turned his horse toward the cafe and rode easily down the street. Milo said something, but it wasn't directed at him.

When Guy dismounted in front of Pack's Eatery, he looked up the street to the Gates residence. The three people were going into the house, probably to discuss the holdup at length. It kind of stuck in his craw that Nicole would have such a man as her betrothed. Milo had a bit of gray at the ears, wasn't especially good-looking, appearing most natural with a scowl on his face, and he was at least fifteen years older than the girl.

Why should Nicole be willing to marry such a man—a man with such a grouchy nature? Of course, to be fair, Guy doubted that any man would be in a good mood after being robbed for the third time in a row.

He dismissed those thoughts, entering the small, cluttered cafe. It was too early for lunch and too late for breakfast, so the place was empty. Empty, that is, except for a gray-haired old-timer standing near a kind of counter. He had more wrinkles in his face than a sun-dried prune, but his eyes were alert and curious. He wiped his hands on the apron around his waist and nodded a greeting.

"Howdy, stranger."

"Good morning...Pack, isn't it?"

"That's me—Pack Johnson."

"I guess it's a little early for lunch, but I kind of missed out on breakfast this morning," Guy said.

"No trouble, long as you've some jingle in your pocket. There seems to be a rash of broke going about. No one wants to pay me for a meal lately."

"No wonder. A man named Benny lost a payroll this morning. A bandit stole his money and even his boots."

"Why would anyone steal Benny's boots?" Pack said.

"Can't say."

"Shucks, Benny's one of the smallest men around. Ain't no one who could wear his boots, less'n it was just a boy."

"I don't know the whys, only what took place."

"So what'll you have for lunch?" Pack asked.

"You got a specialty?"

He grinned, deepening the wrinkles in his face. "I got miner's stew. In that, you get everything but gold dust."

"Bring me a plate of that."

"You didn't strike me as being a man with that much courage right off," Pack chuckled. "Maybe I guessed wrong."

"Looks can be deceiving sometimes," Guy said. "Take you, for instance. You don't look like any ordinary cook."

"No?"

"No. In fact, you look as if you'd be more at ease with a pick or shovel in your hands."

"Think you're smart, do you?" the old-timer said.

"Just an observation. You're tanned and weathered from the sun and elements, you've got calloused hands, and you've got a squint to your eyes that comes from too many hours facing the glare of day."

"I could be just a bit blind."

"You had no trouble picking me out as a stranger."

Pack chuckled again. "I'll get you a plate of

that stew. If you want some fresh meat in it, I'll see if that stray cat is still about."

Guy had to smile. "I'll chance it just the way it is, thanks."

"Then pick yourself a seat, boy. You pretty much got the run of the place, so grab one that I got around to cleaning today."

Guy found himself still grinning at the man as he went back into one corner of the room that served as his kitchen. Guy had the feeling that he would like Pack. He also felt certain that this was the man who'd sent for him. It had been his friend who had been killed, and if he'd sold his mine, he might have had a little money.

Guy sat down in one corner, able to see the door and the only window easily. He decided to feel out Pack about the death of Zack without pinning him down about contacting the detective agency. If he'd wanted to tell the agency who he was, he'd have signed the letter. For the time being, Guy would just play the case by ear.

CHAPTER FOUR

Nicole stood up from the couch, anger leaping into her eyes, her back erect, her hands clenched into fists.

"Don't you lecture me, Milo! You don't have that right—not yet!"

"I'm only saying that it was a fool thing to do, darling," he told her. "Let me set you up here in town. You don't have to live out there among those sheep and take baths in icy mountain ponds. Let me take care of you."

"I can take care of myself," she fired back. "My bakery does a good business. I don't need anyone to support me."

"You know that's not what I meant, darling. I just want to make things easy on you—do things for you."

She said, "And I didn't fall into that man's arms. He was only being a gentleman, helping me off a rather unusual saddle. If he appeared to hesitate, I'm certain he was just making sure I was steady."

"Whatever you say," Milo sighed. "I can't help being jealous of other men. I'm even jealous when you pet your horse or smile at that crazy Pack Johnson. Hell, I'm jealous of the air that gets to touch you as you walk down the street!"

"I've told you not to swear in my presence," she reminded him.

"Sorry, that just kind of slipped out."

Nicole shook her head in dismay. "I sometimes wonder if you were ever around a proper lady, Milo. I'm not one of those girls you talk to in the saloon."

"I know that," he said. "I'm working on it, but my manners will never be that of some high-class gent."

"Simple respect is not that hard to learn. I won't be taken for granted—not now or after we're married."

"Speaking of the wedding, how about I set a date for us?"

"We've only known each other a short while."

"Short while? I've been after you since you come to town two months ago. We've been engaged for more'n a week. How long does this business go on?"

"Most proper engagements last for six months. It gives both the man and the woman time to discover their true feelings toward the other. It saves a good many mistakes."

"I'm not interested in anyone else, darling. What say I set the date for the end of the month?"

"That's three days."

"How about a week then? Two weeks?"

"I don't want to set the date just yet. Can't you be patient?"

"Patient? You haven't allowed me more'n a peck on the cheek in the whole time I've known you! I'm only human, Nicole. You drive me crazy! No wonder my security with the payroll hasn't worked the last three trips. I'm too blasted tied up thinking of you!"

"That's flattering, Milo, even if you say it almost in a rage."

The man let out a frustrated grunt. "I give up. You win. We'll wait until you're ready. I can see that I've got to play your game right to the end, so I'll be patient."

Nicole asked, "What about your men? They might not be so patient about getting paid."

"I gave them what money I had last time

we lost the money. I don't know what else to do. I've got that backup cash coming by stage, so I'll give them all some of what I owe them."

"Are these robberies going to ruin you?"

"We're taking plenty of silver out of the mine right now. The price ain't as high as we'd like, but our yield is pretty good to the ton."

"I don't know much about things like that, I'm afraid," she said.

"I've had this mine for nearly eight years, and it's about to run dry. That little operation I bought from Pack has possibilities, but only time will tell. If the old one runs dry, we'll go into that other hole."

"You were very fortunate to get that first mine."

"Fortunate had nothing to do with it," he said. "Some stinking squatters were nested right on my claim. I had to run them outta the country before I even got a shovel into the ground. This world belongs to the takers, and if you don't take, you'll have people taking from you. It's simply a matter of doing to others first!"

"A rather odd kind of Golden Rule," she said, forcing a lightness into her voice that she didn't feel.

Milo stood next to his big front window,

looking out into the street. Nicole moved over to stand within arm's length of him—as close as she dared.

"Wonder what that man's game is," he said.

"Mr. Kolter?"

"He's over at Pack's."

Nicole said, "Probably just passing through. It almost paid handsome dividends for you. He might have caught that bandit if I hadn't been there to provide the robber a fresh mount."

"I don't like him. There's something about the way he looks at people, as if he's making fun of everyone and everything."

"He didn't strike me that way. He was very helpful and quite the proper gentleman."

"Still, I think I'll have Taco or Ape keep an eye on him," Milo said.

"What could he possibly do that could interest you?"

The man shrugged. "I just don't trust him."

"Is there something you're not telling me, Milo?" Nicole asked bluntly. "If you're covering up your past, or perhaps something that you've done lately..."

"You know all you need to know about me," he snapped. "I'll make you a fine husband. You'll have this house, the finest clothes we can buy, and we'll take a trip to a different city or country every year. I'll show you the world on a silver platter. You'll be treated like a queen."

"I don't need all of those things, Milo. I only need the love and support of a good man, someone I can respect and be proud of."

He let a smile curl his lips. "I'll throw that in for good measure. You'll see, darling. It'll be great."

Nicole saw the passion in the man's eyes, the way he leaned toward her. She turned away from him, retrieving her hat.

"I'd better be getting back. Leroy and Deroy can go out and look for the horse that bandit stole."

"Let me send Flash with you."

"Flash doesn't like the Quinton boys. In fact, no one on your payroll is too fond of them."

"Nobody likes sheepherders," Milo said.

"I do."

He sighed. "Then I'll send Flash and Benny out to try and track that bandit. I'll tell them not to harass your pals."

"Thanks, Milo. They're really very nice."

"You think everyone is nice. I often wonder how anyone grew up so innocent and gullible."

She offered him a warm smile. "Good luck with the bandit, but I imagine you'll find the end of the trail at Skull Mountain again."

"Not much doubt of that, but at least the men will be doing something."

Nicole said, "I'll see you tomorrow for lunch. When is the coach due in?"

"Should be here at midnight—if it don't get robbed or something, too."

"Good day then, Milo."

He opened the door for her, then attempted to kiss her. She was ready for him, carefully turning her cheek toward him. As was his usual reward, he got only a peck on her cheek. Then she was through the door and out of reach.

From his position in the cafe, Guy could see the girl's exit from Milo's house. Nicole didn't really seem to like the man.

When Pack brought out a plate of steaming hot stew, Guy asked him about the couple.

"Odd match, those two," Pack said. "That gal don't seem to be a fortune hunter, but she sure acts like one. That Milo does have the money, but most of it is tied up in other investments. Or so he says."

"Think she's really after some of his worth?" Guy asked.

"Like I said, she don't strike a man that way. But it's hard to believe she loves him."

"She's quite a looker. Funny every man in

the valley isn't after her."

"Milo sees that no one gets too chummy with her. Once she gave Milo a little encouragement, that was the end of any other men courting Nicole."

"What do you think of this bandit?"

"You mean the Skull Mountain Bandit?" Pack said.

"That what they call him?"

"Yup. He plumb disappears up at Skull Mountain after every robbery. I mean this feller don't leave tracks or nothing. He's like a ghost."

"He hit Benny on his way into town as if he knew Benny was coming. You think one of the people in town might be this bandit?"

"Sure couldn't be no stranger, less'n someone is putting him up out there in the hills and selling information. You're the first new face to hit town in better'n a week."

"Seems I heard about some other trouble over here a while back," Guy said. "There was a man killed—I believe he was a friend of yours."

Pack narrowed his gaze. "Zack Lorring was his name. He and I were like brothers."

"You ever find out who killed him?"

"Nope. Even had the sheriff up this way to look into it, but there wasn't a thing to go on.

One shot from a rifle killed him, and he was robbed of what little money he had. The sheriff figures he was robbed by some wandering killer."

"Maybe it was this Skull Mountain Bandit," Guy said.

"No. That jasper has been real careful not to hurt anyone. As I recall, he ain't used his gun once."

"Benny said he carried a sawed-off twin-barreled shotgun. You ever see anyone packing one of those?"

"Can't say that I have," Pack said.

"This fella wasn't too big—from what I could tell in the distance. Fact is, he looked near the same size as Benny."

"Could explain why he took Benny's boots," Pack said.

"What about your friend, Zack? Any reason for someone to kill him?"

"You ask a lot of questions, stranger."

"The handle's Guy Kolter."

"You still ask too many questions. That might not be healthy in this town. Milo don't like people snooping about."

"I don't think me and Milo hit it off all that well that I have to worry about making him like me."

"Cocky, ain't you?" Pack grunted.

"Just curious. I'm doing some speculating for a client. He's interested in Crystal Creek as a location to go into business."

"What kind of business?"

Guy said, "Might be mining. The Gates mine shows a good yield over the past seven or eight years. Could be room for another mining operation here."

"Gates wouldn't allow it," Pack said.

"What do you mean, he wouldn't allow it? How could he stop me from staking claim to some land? I checked the records in Silverton, and there are over twenty homesteads still open. His is the only mining claim recorded there, since you saw fit to sell him your diggings."

"You've been doing a lot of nosing around. You could get that snoot chopped right off."

Guy said, "I don't go out looking for trouble. My work, up to this point, has been to check into Crystal Creek's history. Next I'll be looking over the lay of the land. It would help my findings, though, if this bandit business was cleared up. Also, it doesn't look good on any reports I make if there are unsolved murders in the valley."

"I'd help you if I could on that count, Kolter, but I haven't any real clues."

"How about ideas?" Guy asked.

"Our mine was showing some color. We'd still be making a go of it if Zack wasn't killed."

"And Milo bought your mine?"

"He and all his men had perfect alibis that night. They were in the Big Kitty Saloon having a miners' meeting of some kind."

"Quite a coincidence. Where were you?" Guy asked.

"In town for supplies. I returned to the mine cabin to find Zack lying on his face, a bullet in his back."

"Whereabouts is your mine?"

"Ain't mine no longer, but it's a ways to the east of Gates's mine. Both of them are a couple of miles south of here, near the pass that runs up into the San Juan range."

"Think I'll ride up and look it over. Might find a likely spot to stake a claim or two."

"About the only claim Milo will let you stake is a wooden cross for your burial place."

"You make it sound as if Milo owns this valley."

"Kolter, that's exactly what Milo Gates believes, and he has the men to back up his claim."

Even as Guy had been eating, he'd noticed some activity over at Milo's house. As he put away the last mouthful of stew he could manage, a pair of men walked through the cafe door. They didn't look like the type to make social calls.

CHAPTER FIVE

One of the two men entering Pack's cafe wore a sombrero. He was obviously Mexican, and he wore two guns—both with butt handles forward. He wasn't a small man, but he was dwarfed alongside the other one.

Pack looked the two men over and put on a dark scowl. "Listen now, Taco, Ape, I don't want no trouble here."

"Won't be no trouble." The big man grinned. "We just stopped by to give this stranger some advice."

"That's right neighborly of you," Guy said with a smile. "I didn't know your town had a welcoming committee."

"What committee?" the Mexican asked with

a thick accent, looking at the bigger man.

"We ain't no committee, and we sure enough are not here to welcome you, Kolter," Ape said.

"Then what can I do for you gents?"

"You can get the blazes out of town! We don't want your kind around Crystal Creek!"

"I'd sure be willing to oblige if my horse wasn't worn completely out."

"Trade him at the livery—down the street," the Mexican said. "He'll take your horse straight across for one of his animals."

"Right decent of him," Guy replied, still feinting a friendly attitude. "You don't mind if I finish eating, do you?"

The two looked at one another, as if confused.

Then the bigger one spoke. "You've got ten minutes. Then I'll help you on your way."

"No problem, gentlemen. I'm always happy to comply with the indigenous populace of a town."

"What'd he say?" the Mexican asked.

"He said he's leaving," Ape replied.

That was even a bigger puzzle to Taco. "We ain't going to throw him out?"

The big man put cold eyes on Guy. He was at least six-four in height and probably two-fifty in weight, and it was easy to see why people called him Ape. "Ten minutes, Kolter.

The last minute you get, I'll be coming to help you on your way."

"Don't worry, fellows. I'm sure I can meet your time schedule."

The two of them left the cafe. Guy heard the Mexican complain about not understanding what was going on, but Ape only growled at him.

"Smart move, Kolter," Pack said. "Pack up and git while you can."

"Oh, I'll be back," Guy assured him.

"Back? You heard what they said!"

"They asked me to leave town—so I'll leave. I was meaning to ride out and have a look around, anyway. The switching of horses is a good idea. With Milo's support, I'll be able to trade even. I was expecting to spend an additional ten dollars to get another mount."

"You come back here and Ape will take it personal. I've seen that man in action, son. You don't want any part of him!"

"I'm not the kind of man who looks for a fight, but I do what I want and go where I please. As it happens, I want to go out and look over this Skull Mountain before dark. How about pointing me in the right direction?"

"Four bits for the meal, and the advice is

free. Forget Skull Mountain and keep on riding."

Guy dropped the coins on the table and put on his hat. "See you later, Pack. You won't have to remind me not to order another plate of your stew."

"Should have let me find that stray cat," the man grunted. "I knew that brew needed something special."

By moving quickly, Guy caught up with Nicole five miles out of town. She was taking it easy, for the horse she rode was worn out.

A frown crossed her face as she saw Guy ride up. "I thought that I recognized you following after me."

"Figured that someone ought to watch out for you. Can't tell when that bandit might show up again."

"He isn't after me. I don't carry any money."

"If the bandit has eyes, he might be interested in you for reasons other than money."

"I suppose I could find that flattering, in an offhand sort of way."

"You didn't stay with Milo long. Wasn't he good company today?"

"He was a little put out over losing his money, Mr. Kolter. And you didn't exactly try and lighten his mood. Are you always so insulting to the people you meet?"

"I was jealous," Guy said with a shrug.

"Jealous?"

"Milo has that big house. He owns a producing mine, runs the valley as if he was some kind of king, and he has you trailing after him. I guess I figured he didn't need my friendship —not when he had all of those other things."

"I'm not sure I like your choice of words. I'm not trailing after him."

"You tease him, keep him dangling on a hook for you, but it's you that's doing the chasing. I know about women. You all get a man to chasing after you until he's caught."

"How philosophical you are. But you're wrong."

He cocked an eyebrow at her. "Oh?"

"I'm not a tease."

"You call letting a man kiss you on a cheek— after you're engaged properly to him—not teasing?"

"I'm a proper young lady, Mr. Kolter. I doubt if you can understand that."

"I understand more than you might guess, ma'am."

Now it was Nicole who lifted her eyebrows. "And what is it you understand?"

"That you mean to have Milo on your own

terms. That you want him lapping at your heels like some lovesick puppy, but you're careful to only pat him on the head. You don't love that man, you couldn't respect him, and I sincerely doubt that you'd ever be happy with him as your husband."

Nicole jerked her horse to a stop. Guy did likewise, feeling the heat from her hot, glaring eyes.

"How dare you speak to me in such a fashion! You don't know me at all, Mr. Kolter— and you never will!"

"Why don't you invite me to dinner tonight and give me a chance to apologize?" he said, offering her a good-natured smile.

"Why don't you take a long step off Skull Mountain! I'd like to see how well you bounce!"

"Speaking of that mountain, would you mind pointing it out to me? I'd like to go looking for this mysterious bandit."

She frowned at that. "Why should he interest you?"

"No reason. I'm just a curious sort. I told you that before."

"Your snooping will get you killed! If Flash gets to thinking you're mixed up with the bandit, you'll end up dead!"

"Another of Milo's men?"

"Yes. And he's a bad man to cross. I'm told

that he's killed at least five men in gunfights."

"Men with their back to him or facing him?" Guy asked.

She again darkened with anger. "You're a bigger fool than I might have imagined. What has all of this got to do with you? Why did you come to Crystal Creek?"

"Sorry, that's kind of sociable information. You and I aren't all that sociable just yet. But if I had an invite for dinner, I might just talk my head off to you."

"Milo would have your head for simply asking to dine with me. If you feel like dying, go jump off Skull Mountain, as I suggested in the first place."

"That the big one over there?" He pointed at a mountain whose peak was higher than any of the surrounding hills.

"Yes. The sheep camp is on the lower plains. There's no trail up to the top of Skull Mountain. And when you get to its base, you'll see the reason it's called Skull Mountain. There's a formation of rock about halfway up that resembles a human skull."

"And where is your little cottage from here?" Guy asked.

"You needn't concern yourself with my home. I'm quite safe and sound."

"Living all alone in a land where a bandit is looting and killing?"

"No killings have been blamed on the Skull Mountain Bandit."

"How's your head?" Guy asked, abruptly changing the subject.

"I'm fine, Mr. Kolter. It's your head that should concern you."

He grinned at her. "I didn't think anything was wrong with my head until I first looked at you."

"Oh?"

"Now I'm a mite confused. I'd be glad to be your servant just to be near you."

"How charming," she said dryly, shaking her head in disdain.

"Are you familiar with Shakespeare?"

"He was some writer of plays or something, I believe."

"Uh-huh. And once I read some poems he wrote. I remember some lines about being like a slave to the one you love, thinking of nothing but serving your love, wondering where your love is, never thinking ill of your love, no matter what she does."

Nicole put her horse into motion once more, not speaking a word. Guy kept pace with her, wondering at the girl's cool attitude. He'd always heard that women of all ages liked to hear things from poems even if you didn't know them by heart.

"This is where I leave you," Nicole said as they reached a fork in the trail. "My cabin lies along this path."

"Good day to you then, ma'am. Sorry if my presence annoyed you."

She tipped her head his direction very slightly, then put her horse up the trail that led into the lower hills. She was quickly gone from sight.

Guy let out a sigh. If he ever got around to understanding women, he'd be very surprised.

It only took half an hour to get back to the spot where Benny had been robbed. Guy was now on the same trail he'd ridden previously, stopping at the spot where he'd found Nicole. He looked around, but the ground was rocky, the thick patches of grass and brush hiding any marks. He continued up the steep incline, winding through a maze of purslane, wild rose, and scrub oak.

When he reached the cottonwood and birch trees, he lost all sign of any real trail. He continued working his way higher up, until he reached a plateau. From there, he followed the natural terrain right up to the base of the rocky-faced Skull Mountain.

A deer dashed from the brush, with a fawn right at her heels, then was quickly lost in the heavy foliage. The sounds of the pair moving were audible for a time, but Guy had eyes only for the steep slope. As Nicole had informed him, there was no path up the wall of the mountain.

Guy could see no way to go up the escarpment, so he took his horse along a rocky path in the opposite direction. It would take him toward the sheep camp, some miles away.

There were tracks of deer along the edges of the trail, droppings of rabbits, an occasional elk, and sheep. But Guy could find no prints of a horse, no signs that the trail was used by anything other than animals.

He stopped in a clearing, able to see the mountain behind him more distinctly now. The rocky face did indeed have a stone formation that looked like the skull of a man. But a careful inspection still failed to reveal a way to get up the mountain. It rose like a pillar, almost conical in shape, rocky and impregnable. Standing majestically like a lone sentry, it had a peak that was barren of trees or greenery of any kind. It was the main landmark in sight for many miles.

Far below, two specks were on the main trail. Guy guessed that they were Benny and the gunman named Flash. The only trail they would find was his own.

Guy sat back in the saddle, resting. He rolled a smoke with nimble fingers, thinking things over. As the horse was quiet, not moving, he could hear the distant bleating of sheep. It wasn't far to the camp of the two Quinton brothers. He would get there about suppertime, so he could...

He flipped the cigarette away without lighting it. If he timed it right, he could cadge an evening meal from Nicole. Country courtesy dictated that a person never refused a weary or hungry traveler.

Even as the thought was in his head, Guy was urging his horse down the rough, uneven path. He was certain he could count on the Quinton boys to tell him where the girl's cottage was—provided he was subtle about it.

CHAPTER SIX

The Quintons, as it turned out, were both in camp. They were not very big or tall. In fact, they were about the same size as Guy and, being identical twins, they looked just like each other. They were friendly enough, offering him a meal and lodging for the night.

After speaking to them about the weather, the sheep business, and then mentioning the bandit, Guy found them quite uninformed and closemouthed. Either they knew nothing at all, or they were keeping quiet with what they did know. He bid them farewell once he had wormed the directions to Nicole's cabin out of them.

It was just growing dark when Guy spotted

the lights from a small wooden cabin. With a narrow grin, he turned his horse in that direction.

Nicole was less than pleased to see him. She met him at the door with a gun in her hand. "What are you doing here?"

"Trying to find my way back into town. I saw the lights, but I didn't know it was your house."

"I'll bet," she said sarcastically.

"You wouldn't turn a hungry man out on a cold night without even a decent meal, would you?"

"That would depend on the man. I don't trust you."

"Me?" he said, incredulous. "Why, my mother was a lady! I even have two sisters! I've never harmed a hair on a woman's head in my life!"

"I wasn't concerned about you harming me, Mr. Kolter."

That brought a smile to his face. "You mean, you didn't think you were safe from my numerous charms?"

She continued to block his path, still holding the pistol in her hand. As if to make certain that it was indeed getting dark out, she looked past him at the deepening sky.

"You can't spend the night here."

"I wouldn't think of it," he said quickly. "I wouldn't even consider remaining in your barn. I'm not in the habit of ruining the reputation of innocent young women—especially those with jealous, powerful boyfriends."

"What about my holding a gun on you? That ought to carry some weight."

"It might, if you'd bothered to load the weapon. I'm not easily frightened away by an empty gun," Guy said.

She looked dumbly down at the pistol. "I don't shoot a handgun very often. I suppose I should keep this loaded, what with that bandit running loose."

"Meanwhile"—he took the fragrance that lingered in the air—"could I impose on you for a bite to eat?"

She finally stepped back into the room, allowing him to enter. He removed his hat and waited while she closed the door and put the gun down on the windowsill.

"There's water in the pan, and you'll find a towel next to it, should you care to wash. Supper will be ready in about ten minutes," Nicole said.

He quickly washed up, then took a chair next to the table, watching the girl work. She was as handy in the kitchen as any woman he'd ever seen. When he mentioned it, she paused from her labor.

"That comes from feeding, washing, ironing, mending, and cleaning house for a foster mother and her three boys. I had to become organized or end up without any sleep."

"Sounds like a tough existence. What happened to your parents?"

"They were killed several years ago, murdered over a tiny piece of land. My older brother was killed the same night."

"And you escaped?"

"Not exactly. I was staying with my sick grandmother. When she also died a short time later, I was auctioned off to the first woman who would take me. I earned my keep in that household, slaving away until I was old enough to run away."

"You must have joined up with a baker. You have your own bakery now."

"Something like that," she said.

"So why did you move to Crystal Creek?"

"I like the mountains."

"Colorado is full of mountains. This is kind of an out-of-the-way place to set up shop."

She set a platter of beans and meat on the table, then removed a hot loaf of corn bread from the oven. A pot of tea was soon added to the other things. When Nicole began to sit down, she was surprised to find Guy quickly darting over to hold the chair out for her.

"You think of me as being out of place here, but I daresay I fit in as well as you," she said. "Whatever are you doing in Crystal Creek, Mr. Kolter?"

Before answering, he helped himself from the platter she had passed over to him. "I told you, I'm here on speculation for a client."

"Why your interest in that bandit?" Nicole asked.

"I don't hold with a man who'd hit a woman—let it go at that."

"He didn't really hurt me."

"Falling off your horse, you could have broken your neck or been trampled on. It was no thanks to him that you weren't seriously hurt."

"A poetry lover and now a gallant knight. What other hidden traits do you have in store for me, Mr. Kolter?"

"I'm fond of a good meal." He took a hearty bite of the meat. "I'll be around to cut you some firewood one day soon."

"That isn't necessary."

"Then I'll have to treat you to a meal in town, although I'm not sure that having Pack cook for you would be any treat."

"Pack is a very nice man, but his cooking talents are a bit limited. If you order a steak, though, he doesn't do too badly."

They continued eating in relative silence then, with Nicole making an effort to avoid looking across the table at Guy. He gave most of his attention to the meal, for it was as delicious as anything he'd tasted in weeks.

He finally pushed himself back from the table, satisfied from the feed. He rose as Nicole stood up and offered to help with the dishes.

"Cleaning dishes is not a man's work. Maybe I'll hold you to that stack of firewood, after all, the next time you happen to be out this way."

"Feeding a man a meal as good as that could get him to hanging around every night."

"I'm not making such an offer," Nicole said.

"It's none of my business, and I imagine you'll tell me that straight out, but I have a hard time seeing you attracted to a man like Milo Gates. I don't think you're the kind of woman who could ever be happy with such a man."

"We've already covered that. Maybe you should think of me as a gold digger. I've told you that I had to endure a lot as a child. I don't intend that my children go hungry or get stuck with a foster mother who works them to the bone."

"But then you'll get stuck with having a man like Milo as the children's father."

Nicole bridled instantly, the anger bright in her eyes. "Think whatever you like, Mr. Kolter. I believe you've worn out your welcome."

He picked up his hat and went to the door, but he turned to face her before leaving.

"I'm thankful for the meal, Miss Monday. You'll do some man a real honor by becoming his wife. I'll be envious of that man every time I sit down to a meal."

"Good night, Mr. Kolter. It's eight miles into town. See that you don't get lost on the way."

"I never got lost, ma'am. I've been in a place or two that I didn't recognize right off, and sometimes the world gets turned around the wrong way, but I quickly know where I am."

She didn't speak again, closing the door almost in his face. As he saw it, it would have served him right. He should have kept his mouth shut about Milo Gates. That man was obnoxious, but it was none of his business.

Guy found his horse and carefully set out for town. He hadn't seen any rooming signs anywhere, but there was probably someplace to sleep. If not, he'd try the livery barn.

Something brought Guy awake instantly. He sat up, got his bearings, and crawled to the edge of the loft. He could hear the sounds of men talking outside in excited voices. Before he could climb down, the hostler came into the barn.

"What's happening out there? What's all the ruckus?" Guy asked.

"That blasted bandit hit the stage," the hostler said. "Took only the money of Milo Gates. Didn't no one get a look at him, and he plumb disappeared in the dark. Milo is fit to be tied."

"Seems that our bandit has it in for him personally," Guy said.

"That Milo wants to go out hunting scalps. He thinks that those Quintons are behind the robberies."

"Could they be?"

"They were right here this morning, trading me some mutton for grain. Ain't no way they could have gotten out there to rob Benny."

"You tell Milo that?"

"You hear him shouting, don't you? That's exactly what he's ayelling about. He practically accused me of being in cahoots with them. This stealing is driving that man crazy."

Couldn't happen to a nicer fellow, Guy thought to himself, tipping his hat over his eyes. The smile lingered on his face until sleep overtook him once more.

Pack's breakfast was just a little better than his miner's stew. He simply was not handy around the kitchen. There were only two other men in the cafe for breakfast besides Guy. They seemed capable of devouring whatever was put before them, not paying much attention to its condition or taste.

Guy had forced down as much food as he could handle when a dark form filled the doorway. Ape Mongold was standing there, and he looked primed to take on a grizzly bear, hand to hand. His malevolent eyes were fixed on Guy.

"You don't listen, Kolter. Maybe I'll have to speak in a language you can't help but understand."

"That other horse was a real mess, Ape. I came back to trade for my own roan. Can't fault a man for being partial to his own horse."

Ape wasn't to be put off this time. He took enormous strides across the room. Then he planted himself in front of Guy's table.

"You're a liar, a sneak, and you chase after another man's woman!" Ape roared the words in challenge. "I'm saying that your mother was a dog and your father was a slime devil from the swamp. You're yella clear through, Kolter."

"You left out ugly," Guy told him.

"Yeah, you're ugly as sin and you stink up the place." Ape stood ready, fists the size of watermelons, shoulders the width of a rail-road tie.

"That ought to cover it," Guy said lightly, getting to his feet. "In fact, I'm such a no-good that you shouldn't waste your time on me. No matter what Milo told you, I'm really not worth busting your knuckles for."

"Milo said only to beat..." Ape caught himself and stopped. Then he shook his head. "Take your best shot, Kolter. I'm going to pound you to a bloody pulp and then tie you over your horse. If you live, you'll have better sense than to ever come back here."

Guy's hand flashed to his gun, attempting to draw. But Ape was prepared. He lunged before Guy could get the gun free. The two of them rolled over a table and landed hard on the floor.

Slamming the man with every ounce of strength he could muster, Guy pounded Ape in the face. He got in three good licks before Ape got hold of him and tossed him through the door of the cafe.

Pain exploded in Guy's head. He sought to clear his vision, rolling over, coming to his feet. Ape's powerful fists then banged his ribs and head, causing an array of lights to flash before Guy's eyes. He threw up his hands for protection, trying to ward off the much larger man. It was like trying to hold back the ocean with an umbrella.

Guy grunted from a blow to his body, then felt his teeth rattled by a punch to his face. He countered with several punches, but he was no match for the mountain of a man in front of him. When Guy failed to block a big right hand, his feet went out from under him. He felt the ground hammer at his skull, jolting his senses until he couldn't protect himself. As the black world of unconsciousness consumed him, he thought he heard someone shout.

CHAPTER SEVEN

Guy blinked against the light of day, not knowing if it was even the same day he'd been taken apart by Ape. From the feel of it, some of his parts hadn't been put together in their proper places. He hurt all over. But at least he was on a bed.

After taking a physical inventory, Guy felt that no bones had been broken. The bed was a mere cot in a small, dirty, cramped little room. Someone had covered the walls with cardboard, evidently to keep the wind from whistling through the cracks between the pine boards. The daylight shone through a window—if the square hole in one wall was supposed to be a window.

Other than being put to bed, Guy hadn't been given any attention. The dried blood was still smeared on his chin and his forehead. His shirt was torn down the front, and he couldn't locate his hat. He gingerly swung his legs over the side of the bed and sat up. When the room quit spinning about wildly, he made it to his feet.

Guy found that he was in the back room of the lean-to that served as a cafe. Evidently, Pack had brought him in after the fight, for he certainly hadn't walked under his own power. Using the walls for support, Guy slowly entered the cafe part of the shanty.

"Up already, are you?" Pack asked, coming across to look at him. "Don't seem to me like you're ready yet."

"Who was driving the stage that ran over me?" Guy asked facetiously.

"Ape made short work of you, I'll give him that. Figured you might be a little tougher than that."

Guy moved over to sit down at a corner table. Every breath hurt. His face was so sore that even talking was painful.

"You the one who stopped the fight?" he asked Pack.

"Weren't no fight that I could see," the old-timer said. "If you mean who stopped the beating, it was Nicole Monday. She ran out to save your bacon."

"I'll have to thank her for that."

"You'll do well to avoid her. It's likely that Ape gave you a few punches for chasing after her in the first place," Pack said.

"How about you and me putting our cards on the table face up, Pack. You know that I'm a detective from our Denver office, and I know that you're the one who sent for me. I don't see any point in either of us putting the other one off."

"Well, I'd have told you right off, but I wanted to know if the man they sent me was any good. I figured if you couldn't find out who sent the money and note, you'd not have a chance in the world of finding my partner's killer."

"It wasn't much of a decision, picking you as the man who'd sent for help. But finding Zack's killer might be something else again."

"Not if I tell you who done it. That'd be some help now, wouldn't it?"

Guy narrowed his gaze. "You'll probably tell me that Milo Gates murdered your partner to force you into selling him the mine."

Pack nodded. "You got it, sonny. It was a real load for the two of us to work that mine.

Neither of us could handle it alone. I figure if Zack had gone for supplies that day, I'd have been the one killed instead of him."

"Any clues that have some foundation?" Guy asked.

"None."

"But you think Milo was behind it?"

"I'd bet this here cafe on it."

"Wouldn't be much of a bet," Guy grunted. "That's when I first knew you were the one who'd sent for me—after I tasted your cooking."

"You're feeling better already, ain't you?" Pack said with some sarcasm. "I could have left you lying out there in the street, being an obstacle for passing horses and wagons."

"What can you tell me about this bandit?" Guy said.

"The Skull Mountain Bandit?"

"Unless you've got more than one running loose."

"Maybe I should give you a little history on Crystal Creek," Pack said.

"That'd be good for openers."

"Right after the Utes were kind of relocated, miners came through these hills. About the same time, there were a few nesters and even some honest homesteaders moving through.

One family named Roberts even settled with
their house not a hundred yards from where
Gates set up his claim. Seems that family was
murdered by some renegade Utes—although
no one ever proved it was Indians."

"Convenient for Gates," Guy said.

"That was about seven or eight years back.
Me and Zack arrived shortly after the mining
began and staked our own claim. While the
Gates operation grew bigger and he hired on
more men, me and Zack just kept plugging
away on our own."

"Any other miners come in?" Guy asked.

"They always met with misfortune of some
kind—if'n you get my drift. There were cave-
ins, beatings, and more than one wagonload
of ore lost to the steep mountain grades. It
was usually enough to drive any other pro-
spectors out."

"Why do you think that no one bothered you
and Zack until just recently?"

"From the sounds of it, the Gates mine is
running into more solid, poor-grade ore all the
time. He keeps telling everyone how high his
silver content is, but I don't swallow it. I think
he needed our mine to expand in. I think
they've hit so much hard rock that they can't
make money in his mine. Ours still has a lot
of silver left in it."

"What'd he pay you for your mine?" Guy asked.

"Two thousand dollars so far and one percent of the take. And he still owes me a five-hundred-dollar payment. I figure my time will run out about the time he starts hauling ore from my diggings. Milo ain't the kind to share his wealth."

"What about this bandit thing?"

"I'm getting to that, sonny. Keep your torn shirt on," Pack said.

"Sorry."

"The valley stayed on an even keel for several years. The sheepmen came in a half a year ago. Or a little more. Then Miss Monday opened a bakery and started seeing Milo regularly. The saloon grew a mite, with a couple shady dudes always picking up any loose change that's floating around. Six weeks or so back, that bandit made his first appearance. He's hit Milo hard and steady—even to getting the stage last night."

"I heard some of the ruckus. Pretty gutsy, holding up a stage by himself."

Pack said, "He dropped on the coach from a tree, took the money only for Milo Gates, and then made them stop long enough to get off. It all took place without the passengers even knowing the robbery had taken place."

"How long after your partner was killed before this bandit put in his first appearance?" Guy asked.

"No connection there, sonny. The bandit had robbed twice before Zack was murdered. Milo blamed the killing on the Skull Mountain Bandit, but I know better. That guy's been real slick so far, but he hasn't harmed a soul."

"What do you know of those Quinton boys?"

"Not enough to vouch for them, but they were in town during the holdup of Benny."

"And the saloon? What about those guys?"

"Riley would be my guess, if it's someone from the saloon. He's a slippery-fingered son, always winning on long odds. He has a show of money, and he's often out of town without reason. Some claim he has a girlfriend over in Silverton, but I've no one to verify that."

Guy said, "This bandit could be one of Milo's men. What about them?"

"The miners never get time enough to set up anything—less'n they have a man working with them. They put in twelve hours a day, except for Sunday."

"There were two holdups on Sunday."

"I've served those men in here. They aren't the type to get mixed up in anything like that," the old man said.

"And his gunhands?"

"Flash Tokat is his main man, but he's loyal enough. Then there's Benny, Ape, and Taco. Those four do most of the dirty work for Milo."

"You've eliminated every man except Riley."

"I didn't take myself off of that list. I could be the bandit," Pack said.

"I admit you're about the right size, and you probably sit a horse like a sack of grain, but I don't see you agile enough to be jumping onto coaches from trees."

"Smart one, ain't you?"

"That's what got all my teeth loosened. Maybe I'll play dumb from here on."

"What are you going to do now?"

Guy said, "Get cleaned up first off. Tomorrow I'll repay a debt. But before then I'll make a trip over to the saloon. I'd like to get a little closer to this Riley fellow."

"What about Ape?" Pack asked.

"I won't be close enough for him to swing at, should we square off again. If I have to plug both his legs to stop from being beaten to death, I'll do just that."

"How are you going to get any evidence against Milo?"

"If he did kill Zack Lorring, I'll figure a way to get a confession out of him or his killers."

"Just like that, huh?"

"Just like that," Guy replied. "Where can I wash up and change clothes?"

"I've a basin out back. Should be a water barrel with plenty of water for cleaning up."

"Thanks, Pack. I'll see if my body works, and I'll get to looking human again."

"I've got to start supper. Want me to fix you something?"

"I don't feel much like eating, Pack. You tend to the unfortunate souls who come through the front door. They're going to have to pay for your culinary abuse."

"Bah!" Pack grunted, turning toward his stove. "I should have left you in the street. I get no thanks, no consideration—only gripes about my cooking. Should have married that old Ute squaw last winter. Maybe everyone'd be happy eating roots, grubs, and raw fish."

Guy didn't listen to any more, making his way out the back of the cafe. The cold water would not only clean him up, it would put some life back into him. He couldn't afford the time to sit around and recover properly. There were things to do, places he had to look over, people he needed to see. Thinking of Nicole stopping Ape from using his face as a broom and sweeping the street with it, he knew he would particularly enjoy seeing her.

• • •

Riley was not a talkative sort. He was the
kind who played his cards close to the vest
and never looked at his hole card twice. He
was slight of build for a man, had delicate
hands from never doing any hard work, and
allowed no expression to enter his face.

Guy spent most of the evening watching
him, then sat in for a time in a card game with
the gambler. Riley was cool, never showing
any nervousness, not even with a flick of his
eyes. Trained and practiced as a gambler, the
man was well suited to his trade. It was near
closing before the two of them were left alone
at the table.

"All right, Kolter," the gambler said, "I've
played enough cards to know when I'm the
hole card that you're interested in. What's on
your mind?"

"I'm looking for a way to get even with Milo
Gates. Word has it that he doesn't own you,
like he does the rest of the town."

"I'm my own man, but I'm not apt to buck
Milo or his men. When you play the odds, you
don't buy in against that kind of game."

"A couple of smart men might just be able
to break him and his whole operation," Guy
said.

"More likely, they'd both get themselves
killed. The men on that man's payroll aren't

squeamish when it comes to a fight. You ought to know that firsthand."

"That bandit is hitting Milo pretty hard. Maybe we could team up with him."

"You know who it is?" Riley asked.

"I've a pretty good idea," Guy bluffed.

"Then you ought to talk to him, not me. I make my living with cards, not with a gun and hood. You want a piece of Milo Gates, you had best buy your spot in the cemetery first."

"Might make you a wealthy man, Riley. You could even set up your own casino in Denver or some big city back East."

"You're tracking the wrong buck, my friend. I'm content to fleece these miners for my living. I don't need a big casino and all the worries that go with it."

"You could take that gal from Silverton and show her the world," Guy said.

That brought a reaction from the other man. His eyes narrowed at once, a cold light glowing in them. He gathered in the cards and stuck them into his vest.

"Game's over, Kolter," Riley said. "You'd better do your snooping someplace else. I don't like the rules you're outlining."

"Were I betting more than just one hand, Riley, I'd say that you're stuck in Crystal Creek because you have a price on your head. You can't leave your girl behind, but you can't get enough money ahead to take her away from Colorado, either. You have to hide out in these little settlements because you won't risk being seen by a lawman."

The gambler's face showed no emotion again. "You're guessing blind, Kolter, tossing cards to see where they land. If you think there's a bounty on my head, why not try to take me in and collect it?"

"Like I said, I only want to get back at Milo Gates. You help me, and I'll make it worth your while."

"No deal." The man shook his head. "I'm not bucking odds like that for any amount of money."

Guy stood up, convinced that he'd been right in most of his guesses, but still unable to tell just how much Riley knew or if he was involved in the holdups. For Riley might have nothing to do with the robberies. He might simply be a man on the run, wanting to hide, but also wanting to be close to the woman he loved. To hide from the law, he circulated in the small mining camps, scraping together what money he could from miners. Once he had a sizable stake, he would likely take his girl and leave the country.

On the other side of the coin, Riley could be

the bandit, getting himself a small fortune in cash from his holdups. He could acquire the money much more quickly that way, and he wouldn't have offered to take on any partner. After all, the bandit was doing fine on his own. By being at the saloon, keeping his ears open, he could have heard the news about the different payrolls. Riley was in a good position to simply absorb information and bide his time.

Heading over to the hayloft to spend another night, Guy reasoned that he was no closer to finding the bandit than he'd been before. Pack thought that Milo had killed Zack Lorring, but there was no proof. Somehow Guy had to get that proof.

CHAPTER EIGHT

Guy had been cutting firewood for over an hour. The exercise seemed to loosen up the stiff, sore muscles. By now he'd piled up enough wood to last for several weeks. Fortunately, someone else had pulled all the dead trees and scrap timber over to Nicole's cabin. He only had to cut the wood into pieces and stack it against the side of the place.

He stopped work at last, sweating from the exertion, out of breath. He'd removed his shirt, for he didn't want to stain it with sweat. As there was a watering trough handy, he rinsed himself off—arms, face, chest—then toweled himself with the cloth he carried in his saddle-bags.

Removing his timepiece, he wondered at Nicole's not returning home. It was growing late, and she should have closed the bakery a while ago. It was likely that she'd stayed in town to visit her beau, the tyrant of the valley, Milo Gates.

That thought irked Guy. No woman could be that blind, or could let money be that important to her! He couldn't comprehend why a woman like Nicole would have anything to do with a big-mouth, swaggering oaf like him. Despite her own words, Guy did not believe she was a gold digger.

He donned his shirt and strapped on his gun. He took a last look around, feeling that he was not as alone as he seemed to be.

The air was still, except for the distant hammering of a woodpecker and the chatter of a disturbed chipmunk. He shook off the feeling and mounted his horse. He had a mind to look over the Quintons. As their camp was not far off, it wasn't difficult to pay them a visit.

Nicole watched the man turn his horse through the trees, hitting the trail that led up to the sheep encampment. Even though she was completely sheltered by the thick growth of oak shrubs, Nicole sensed that Guy Kolter might *feel* her presence. She didn't know why, but she preferred not to face the man. He was too . . . too virile, too enthralling. Not only didn't she trust what he would do around her, she feared what she might do around him.

She had stood in the shadows, watching the man work. Even from the distance, she could see the dark blotches against his lean-muscled frame. Ape had battered him about like a rag doll, and still the man was up and chopping wood already. He was resilient, and he certainly hadn't been frightened away from her. Milo would be furious to learn of Guy's visit — providing anyone told him.

Going back to gather in the reins of her horse, Nicole led her animal up to the small corral. She had to admire the stack of wood against the cottage, for it would last her a good portion of the summer. When Guy paid for a meal, he did one fantastic job.

Once inside the cabin, she began to wonder what Guy would do. It was obvious that he'd headed up to have a talk with the Quintons — although she didn't know why. He was more than just a speculator, but what exactly was he? The only clue she had was seeing the way Pack took him in after his beating.

If he was a friend of Pack's, he could be trouble for Crystal Creek. The only thing the old ex-miner really cared about had been his

lifelong friend, Zack Lorring. When he'd been
killed, Pack had seemed to die with him. In
fact, the first spark of life she'd noticed in the
old man was when he'd gone out and dragged
Guy Kolter off the street. She'd gone to help
him, but he'd pushed her to the side.

"Don't need none of Gates's friends to help!"
he'd snapped at her.

Nicole felt a warm flush of shame creep up
her throat. Pack had felt that Ape had beat
up Guy because of her. It could well have been
the case. Milo had been jealous of the man at
once, and she'd inadvertently mentioned that
she'd given the man a meal. Milo hadn't
seemed visibly upset, but Guy had paid the
price later that same morning. She might have
been partially responsible.

There was a chill in the air, with clouds
gathering overhead. Nicole started a fire at
once, taking advantage of the new pile of wood.
She didn't want muscles like a man, or calloused hands, so she always hated the job of
cutting firewood. It was a pleasant luxury to
heat up the cottage early.

Thinking over what she would prepare for
supper, she decided to put forth some effort.
There was a good chance that Guy would stop
back by after his visit to the Quintons. That
thought sent an odd shiver up her spine, a

fluttering within her stomach. It was a ridiculous situation. She was hoping he'd stop by for supper, yet afraid of being around him. Whatever he was up to, it meant trouble for her and the valley.

Even as that thought filtered through Nicole's head, she was busily preparing to bake some fresh rolls. He'd surprised her the last time he'd come for a meal. This time, she would show him what a real cook could do.

Leroy and Deroy were not the most sociable men Guy had ever run across. They skirted his questions, avoiding direct answers, and were more than a little distant toward him. They were identical twins, both with the same light beard around the points of their chins. As they were dressed in matching woolen coats, it would have been hard to tell them apart from any distance.

"What can you tell me about your neighbor, Miss Monday?" Guy asked the one called Leroy.

"What's to tell?"

"With a bandit running loose, shouldn't you keep an eye on her?"

The man shrugged. "The bandit don't bother anyone but Milo Gates. Why should he bother the girl?"

"She and Gates are engaged to be married.

That bandit might decide to get at Milo through Miss Monday," Guy said.

Leroy looked at his brother for help. "What do you think, Dee?"

"This fella is snooping for something special, Lee. Maybe we ought to come right out and ask him just what that is."

"All right, Kolter," Leroy said. "What is it that you're after?"

Guy offered the two men a grin of defeat. "You got me cold there, boys. I'm not looking for the bandit at all. I'm more interested in a man named Zack Lorring. You remember him?"

"We sold him a mutton on occasion. Him and Pack used to have the claim over toward Gates's silver mine. Don't know much else."

"No ideas who might want him dead?"

"Anyone who wanted the mine, I suppose. Word is that the two of them—Zack and Pack—were hitting better ore than even Gates," Leroy said.

"You ever have any trouble with Gates or his crew?"

"They leave us alone, and we leave them alone," Deroy said. "This fall we'll sell the herd and move back to Kansas. We ain't too concerned about anything that happens in this valley, long as no one bothers us."

"Does Nicole come up to visit you often?"

"She works in town. We swap some venison or mutton with her for some fresh bread or rolls sometimes. Other than that, we don't see much of her."

"We did return her saddle," Leroy added. "Found the horse up on the mesa the day after the bandit stole Benny's money and boots."

"Anything else left with the horse?" Guy asked.

"Just the saddle and bridle. Could be that the bandit turned the horse loose and it naturally came back to where we'd been feeding him."

"Then you returned the saddle to Nicole Monday already?" Guy said.

"Yesterday."

"We got the bandit's horse, so how does he get around?" Guy asked.

"He obviously has more than one animal stashed back in the hills someplace."

Guy decided that he'd get nothing more out of the two brothers. He bid his farewell to them and rode out of their camp. Once down into the trees, he turned to look back. The two men were going about their business, not paying him any attention at all.

The two men could have used deception to make the hostler think they were both in town

during a holdup. After all, a change of coat
and hat, a wave or word as they spoke, and
no one would know which brother had walked
past them. Unless someone could verify seeing
them both at the same time, it was a workable
theory. The problem was, it was only an idea,
a thought—and connected to the Skull Mountain Bandit. That wouldn't do him any good,
for he was being paid to find the murderer of
Zack Lorring, not the bandit himself.

Dropping down to the same trail he'd followed up into the hills, Guy let his animal
pick his own pace. The light was dim. It would
be dark in an hour.

He had about decided not to trouble Nicole
when he caught the scent of something delicious and enticing floating in the air. He went
so far as to stop his horse, looking toward the
girl's cottage.

Her door was open, the smell of freshly baked
goods radiating through the whole outdoors.
Only a man of iron could have passed up such
a fragrance. Guy was not that man of iron.

He rode up to the pole corral, noticed the
odd-looking saddle that was made for a woman,
then looked over the big black mare. Milo had
called her Midnight and it was appropriate.
There was not a speck of white on the animal

anywhere, and her coat was as dark as a hunk of coal.

Before Guy could dismount, a figure appeared at the doorway. Nicole had her apron around her waist and a light, airy blouse of soft yellow over a dark-gray skirt. The apron was white, trimmed with lace. He was struck at the sight of her, for she was much more feminine than he'd thought. Her hair was pulled back just enough to keep it out of the way while she worked, the light-brown curls caressing her shoulders.

"Why, Mr. Kolter," she said. "Fancy finding you way out here at this time of the evening."

"Fact is, I was fifty miles away just a few minutes back," he teased. "The sweet scent of your cooking carried that far. Wonder I didn't run my horse to death getting here."

"Come in, when you're ready. I was just about to check the venison on the stove. Good thing you got here when you did."

He watched her go back inside, then loosened the cinch on his horse and let him drink at the trough. Guy didn't figure on staying long, so he didn't bother picketing him where he could graze.

As Guy entered the small cabin, Nicole gestured toward a chair. He barely sat down before she served up a plate of hot rolls and honey.

"You can start on those. I have some boiled cabbage on the stove and baked potatoes. The steak should be ready in five minutes."

"It might be the suspicious nature of a man like myself, but this looks like a meal that was intended for company."

She flashed him a smile. "Let's just say that it's payment for services rendered. I hate chopping wood."

"I owed you that."

"No, you didn't. The last time you ate here, it was an act of courtesy. This meal is my personal thanks for doing a chore for me. There is a big difference."

"I won't argue with you about it, but I doubt that your fiance would see it that way. You figuring on getting me another stomping on by one of his men?"

She flicked an uncomfortable glance his direction. "I—I'm sorry about that. I didn't know that he intended to sic Ape on you."

"I'm beholden to you for stepping in on my behalf. I wasn't doing much good against him."

"He's twice your size. It's a wonder he didn't kill you before I intervened."

"Why did you get involved at all?" Guy asked.

She took out the baked potatoes, set them on the table, and began to stir some flour and milk for gravy. Her eyes remained on her work, as if she didn't want to look his direction.

"First, Mr. Kolter, you tell me something."

"What?"

She put her eyes on him now. "Why are you here in Crystal Creek?"

"I told you, I'm—"

"Please don't insult my intelligence, Mr. Kolter. Who are you working for and what are your goals?"

He sighed, slicing a hot potato in half. "I work for a detective agency in Denver. I was hired to look into a murder."

"Zack Lorring's?" Nicole asked.

"That's right."

"Then you have no real interest in the Skull Mountain Bandit, only in the death of Pack's partner."

"More or less."

"You mean that you think the bandit might have killed Zack?"

"It's possible, but it doesn't seem likely... unless..."

"Unless what?"

"Unless Milo isn't making any money out of his mine right now. He might have this bandit working for him."

Nicole tested the steak and set the cabbage on the table. She worked quickly to prepare the gravy and then put a large steak on a plate for Guy.

"Good thing Ape didn't knock my teeth out. I'd have been real put out, not being able to tie into something as appetizing as the meal you've provided."

That brought a wisp of a smile from Nicole. She sat down, preparing her own plate, not speaking again until they were both eating.

"Why would the bandit work for Milo?" she asked.

"If Milo's getting robbed, no one can expect to get paid. If he can hold on until his men get going into Pack's mine, then he'll have some more money coming in."

"You think the robberies are only a cover-up for Milo being out of money to pay his hired help?"

"It's possible."

"Am I to conclude that you think Milo killed Zack Lorring?" she asked.

He lifted a shoulder carelessly. "I work on supposition, but only facts will dictate who the killer was. I don't suppose you'd care to put me on a clear track."

"I don't talk business with Milo. If you expect me to inform on him, you're less of a

gentleman than I suspected. At any rate, I'd
be of no help to you. Milo keeps his work to
himself."

"All right, I'll not impose on your hospital-
ity. But I have leveled with you on my reasons
for being in Crystal Creek. I was hired to find
a killer. In turn, I'd like you to be honest with
me."

"You mean about Milo and myself?" she said.

"That's right. Why is a beautiful, charming,
great little cook like you chasing after such a
ruthless man?"

"I should remind you that you only have
your suspicions about Milo. No one has come
forth with any evidence against him. You're
convicting him without so much as a hearing."

"All the same, what do you find so attractive
about him?"

"He treats me like a lady. He's quite charming when he puts his mind to it, and his future
is secure."

"Being rich, you mean?" Guy asked.

She frowned at that. "Do you know what it's
like to be dirt poor? Have you gone to bed
wanting to cry nights for the ache in your
stomach that you can't fill? Have you watched
your baby sister wither away and die at three
weeks of age because your mother hasn't any
way to feed her?"

"Can't say that my family was that bad off, thank God."

"And thank Him you should," she said with some fire. "Before my parents and brother were killed, I knew what that kind of poor was like. That's the main reason I was glad to wait on my dying grandmother. It was better than going to bed hungry every night."

"You said something about them setting up a homestead."

She laughed without humor. "They knew nothing of being farmers. My father didn't even have a plow. He'd worked in a factory for fifty cents a day before he got that homestead. He didn't even have sense enough to know that a person couldn't farm above eight thousand feet."

"Then they were doomed to failure," Guy said.

"My father was the kind of man who doomed his entire family to failure, Mr. Kolter. He liked to drink occasionally, and it usually was at work. I can't count the number of times he came home early, having been fired from some job. He had no ambition, until he got that homestead. He thought that getting free land would make him a wealthy man, but it was just another of his dreams. If he hadn't gotten himself, my mother, and my brother killed that way, they'd probably have starved to death."

"Sounds like a real prize of a man."

"Don't get me wrong. He was a wonderful, loving man. He simply didn't have a knack for getting ahead in the world. No one mourned the death of my little sister more than he."

"So you think you can give up things like love, respect, and kindness as long as there's enough money around."

That struck a nerve. Nicole rose from the table, beginning to clear away the dishes. As Guy stood to give her a hand, she shook her head.

"I told you that I didn't need any help in my kitchen."

"Sorry, sometimes I can't help being polite," he said.

"It's getting quite late. If someone were to see you leave here, you'd likely get a worse beating than Ape gave you."

"I won't take another beating, Miss Monday. I might get killed, but it won't be by the hands of some overgrown bear of a man."

She moved to open the door for him. He picked up his hat, but stopped next to her, close enough to detect the scent of the mild perfume.

He said, "You were ready for me tonight,

and I don't mind telling you, I've never had a finer meal. I can only wonder why you went to so much trouble."

"Maybe I was just feeling sorry for you. I kind of feel responsible for the beating you took."

"I'd take a beating like that every day of my life, for just a single good-night kiss from your sweet lips."

That shocked her. She leaned back, as if frightened that he would forcibly kiss her. The color rose in her cheeks.

He grinned at her reaction. "Of course, I'll have to wait until my face heals up. I've still get a bit of swelling from Ape trying to loosen my teeth."

Nicole didn't reply but remained pressed against the wall until he was out of the cottage. He took several steps, then looked over his shoulder at her.

"Good night, Miss Monday. Thanks again for the most delicious meal of my life."

"Good night, Mr. Kolter," she returned, her voice steady but a little more husky than usual.

CHAPTER NINE

Something slammed into the pommel of the saddle, the jolt nearly knocking the horse off his legs. The blast of a gun sounded in the night at nearly the same instant.

Guy rolled out of the saddle as his spooked horse ran a short distance away. As Guy hit the ground, he crawled quickly off the trail, scooting into a stand of brush. His gun was in his hand, eyes searching the darkness.

He listened intently, trying to slow his pounding heart, holding his breath for silence. There was a good chance that whoever fired would think that he hit him, for only the front of the saddle had protected him. The ambusher would be wary, though, for he couldn't know how badly Guy was hit. He would want to check him first, try to get close without...

The sound of grass crunching underfoot turned Guy's attention to a small section of birch trees. He couldn't see very clearly, for the moon's light did not penetrate the sheltered trail. But he could distinguish movement. The shadowy figure was working his way forward, a rifle in his hands.

Guy aimed his pistol. He had a clear shot, for the man was between the trees now. Guy could knock him down with a single shot.

"Hold it!" Guy shouted. "Drop the rifle or die!"

The man reacted at once, swinging his gun toward Guy's position. He fired in nearly the same motion, the bullet thudding into the ground only inches in front of Guy's face.

By the time Guy returned fire, the man was in the trees, making his way toward his waiting horse. Up on his feet, Guy gave chase, running a zigzag course, in case the man tried to get off another shot. Guy was too slow, for he heard the pounding of hooves. He'd let the man get away.

Stopping to catch his breath, Guy cursed himself for not taking his shot. The man had tried to kill him from ambush. He deserved no warning, no chance to surrender or maybe get off a lucky shot and finish the job he'd started. Guy should have fired first and questioned the corpse later.

As he made his way back to pick up his horse, he was filled with the same self-doubts he'd known after the death of his partner. When dealing with a deadly killer, you had to shoot fast. Maybe he'd remember that next time.

It was good that he'd gotten his own horse back, for a rented animal would have headed for town and his home at the livery stable. Guy's own mount had run only a short way, then stopped. By speaking to him in a coaxing voice, Guy was able to walk right up to him.

Once headed back into town, Guy asked himself who had ambushed him. Was it the Zack Lorring killer, worried that he was getting close, or was it jealous Milo Gates, angry that he'd dared go see his woman a second time?

He rode up a small canyon and found a place to camp for the night. He didn't want to ride into town, after all, and give the bushwhacker a second chance to kill him.

"There he is," Jeff Portt whispered. "Let's take him!"

"He might not be alone. We should check him first," Guy said.

"Come on, Guy! The man is alone. We can handle him. Just follow me!"

Guy kept pace with Jeff, going up the street, closing the distance between themselves and the man suspected of robbing a Cherry Creek bank. Their prey seemed wary. Guy felt they'd been discovered.

He took hold of Jeff's arm. "Look out! He's going to—"

The man spun toward them, drawing his gun. Even as he fired, Guy was going for his own gun. He returned fire before the man could get off a second shot, but Jeff was falling at his side.

His own bullet hit their suspect high in the shoulder, but it was enough to knock him down. Guy rushed over to kick away the man's gun, then returned to Jeff. He dropped to his knees, lifting his friend's head, trying to stop the blood flow from a wound in his chest.

"Jeff! Why didn't you wait! Why'd you risk this!"

His partner's head rolled, his eyes filled with pain, his life's blood running onto the ground. He coughed, unable to speak. Then his body went rigid. He was dead.

"It's your fault, Guy," a voice said through the fog. "You were fast enough to beat that man to the draw. You should have drawn your gun. You should have been ready to kill him on the spot. It's your fault, Guy. You could have saved Jeff. You could have saved Jeff...."

Guy's eyes sprang open; his body was drenched in a cold sweat. He found that he was sitting up, his arms cradling his blanket. It had only been another dream—the familiar nightmare of that fateful gunfight. He shook his head, wishing the churning within his stomach would stop, mopping the sweat from his forehead. He couldn't shake the vision of Jeff's face, the hurt and anguish that had shown in his eyes, the way he'd died with unspoken words on his lips.

Was the voice in the fog right? Could he have saved Jeff's life? If he had grabbed his gun—instead of Jeff's arm—could he have shot the suspect before Jeff was hit?

He could never truly know the answer to his nightmarish questions. The arm he'd grabbed was Jeff's left arm, not his friend's gun hand. If Jeff had been quicker to react, perhaps he could have saved himself. Why hadn't Jeff drawn his own gun? Could Jeff have frozen in that instant of time?

Guy took a look around. It was barely daylight, and it appeared that nothing else in the world was stirring at that hour. So he built a fire and put on coffee. He doubted that the attacker from the previous night was still around. Even if he had remained out in the dark, he wouldn't know where Guy had gone to. By the time he discovered the fire and smoke, he would be too late to get a second chance at Guy. Besides, this time Guy was alert.

He wasn't really hungry, after such a feed at Nicole's house, so he drank a cup of coffee, warmed himself by the fire, then struck camp. There were some questions he intended to put to some of the people of Crystal Creek. But first he would take a ride up to the mines. If Milo's diggings were about to run dry, it would surely put the suspicion on him for Zack's murder.

"Fine thing," Milo was complaining. "Every man jack of them walked out of the mine yesterday. If I don't pay them what I owe them by the end of the week, they'll move out of Crystal Creek!"

"What can you do?" Nicole asked sympathetically.

"I'm sending Flash, Benny, and Taco with what ore I have. They'll bring back payment for the last couple of shipments. I'll also send a note to the bank in Silverton to give them what money I have left. It should about cover the men's wages."

"Sounds like you've about hit bottom."

"I've run as dry as my silver mine, darling. If I don't hit good ore inside of week, working Pack's old diggings, I'm going broke."

"That is distressing. If you go under, Crystal Creek will dry up like those other short-term mining towns."

"It ain't happened yet. Ape is going to run the crew as of tomorrow. Those miners will either work or he'll knock some sense into them."

"Like he did to that stranger in town, Guy Kolter?"

Milo shrugged. "The man's nothing but trouble. He's been snooping around. I don't know what he's up to, but I don't like it."

She said, "Ape worked him over pretty good, but it didn't stop him. I don't think Mr. Kolter is the kind of man you can stop with threats."

"Then I'll stop him with a bullet!"

"Listen to yourself, Milo! That man hasn't done one blessed thing to you, and you're talking about killing him! What's gotten into you?"

"It ain't me that I'm concerned about," Milo said. "I don't like him sniffing around you, chasing after you as if you were free. What's mine is mine!"

"We are not married yet, Milo Gates! You'd best remember that!"

"We're as good as married," he countered. "You gave me your word. You said that you'd marry me!"

"An engagement can be broken," she warned. "It's not the same as a marriage."

"A damn waste of time, if you ask me!"

"You're swearing again," she reminded him.

"So what if I am?" he shouted. "Ain't I got the right to get mad as blazes about what's been happening to me? That dirty son of a snake that robs only me, the mine drying up, and now you're giving me a hard time. If that don't make a man mad enough to swear, I don't know what would."

"Any person with brains can express himself without vulgar language. If you can't have decency for yourself, have some respect for me."

Milo clenched his fists and stormed about the room, his face red with rage. When he stopped, it was to look out of the front window of his house. That did little to lighten his mood, for Guy Kolter was dismounting at the gate.

"Here comes your dinner guest," he growled. "You sure were eager to invite him for a second time."

Nicole rose to stand next to Milo. "How'd

you know about Guy having dinner at my place again?"

"Flash and Benny thought they was following the bandit, but it turned out to be your pal. Too bad Flash and Benny wasn't invited for supper as well. I'm sure they and Kolter would have given you some lively conversation."

"I don't like to be spied on, Milo."

"And I don't like being made a fool of, Nicole," he snapped.

"Meaning?"

"Just what I said. I figure the only one you should invite out to dinner is me. Being that *I'm* the one you're engaged to. I don't want you to see or talk to anyone unless I say it's okay."

Nicole stood squarely up to the man, even though he towered over her. Her own temper had been brought to surface now.

"You can think what you like, Milo Gates. Our engagement is off—as of now!"

He started to speak, but she pushed past him. She opened the door with such a shove that it nearly smacked into Guy. Without looking in his direction, she stormed out of the yard.

CHAPTER TEN

Guy reached to tip his hat, but Nicole went past him without so much as a sidelong glance. He couldn't help but notice the way she marched through the gate and kicked it shut. She crossed toward her bakery, but there was no lightness to her steps, none of her usual gaiety. She practically stomped her feet on the wooden porch, then slammed her door behind her.

"Now what the devil do you want, Kolter?" Milo demanded. "I'm talking to you, meat-head!"

Guy slowly turned to look at the man. He had to grin, for Milo's face was red, the blood boiling just beneath the surface. It appeared

102

Nicole had finally come to her senses about their engagement.

"I can come back later, Gates, if you're having a fit. Hate to keep you from something as beneficial as that."

"Ape should have smashed your face in harder. You never learn, do you, Kolter?"

"I'm beginning to catch on. I see that Nicole also got wise to your game. Good for her."

"You're asking to get stomped again. Maybe I'll do it myself this time," Milo said.

"You don't look as tough as Ape. Better call him to do your fighting for you . . . like last time."

Milo put his hands on his hips. "Why are you here, Kolter? I'm getting fed up with you chasing after my woman and snooping around town. Just what kind of game are you playing?"

"I work for the Denver Detective & Armed Escort Agency, Gates. I'm investigating a murder, and you're my number-one suspect."

That darkened Milo's face even more, the veins on his forehead bulging as if they were about to explode. When he spoke, he hissed the words through clenched teeth.

"You'd best get out of Crystal Creek, Kolter. I only had Ape work you over. Next time, I'll let him kill you."

"Sorry, Gates, but there's only one beating to a suspect. You send Ape after me again, and I'll have to stop him with a bullet. Then I'll come after you as an accomplice to attempted murder. Not quite the charge I have in mind for you, but it would get you behind bars for a time."

"A detective don't have no authority to arrest anyone, Kolter. If you end up dead, no one will even wonder why."

"You keep on thinking like that—one of your men did last night. My saddle stopped the bullet meant for me. Your boys are a bunch of foul-ups. That's why I'll find the information I need to pin the murder of Zack Lorring on you. Too many mistakes, too dumb—no wonder they're working for you!"

"I should have worked you over myself, instead of letting Ape have that pleasure. It would feel real good to bruise my knuckles on your face."

"You aren't Ape," Guy told him shortly. "You may be bigger than me, but you're not tougher. You're just a bully with a big mouth."

Milo came down from the porch, his fists raised, a rage in his face. "You've just opened your mouth for the last time, Kolter. You chased after my woman until she turned on me, and now you're sticking your nose into my private affairs. That's it! You just bought your-self a plot in our cemetery!"

Guy was ready, ducking under the bigger man's vicious first swings. Unlike Ape, Milo was not an experienced fighter. He threw his weight into wild punches that got nothing but air.

Slipping under the man's guard, Guy stung him in the face with a sharp left, ducked away from a wicked right, then punished Milo with a solid right hand to his face. Guy danced away, only to stop again, slamming a left-right combination into the man's midsection.

Milo was grunting, his anger turning to exhaustion rapidly. He was totally frustrated, trying to hit the elusive Guy. Ape had handled Guy with no trouble, but Milo couldn't even land a punch.

Guy straightened Milo with an uppercut to his jaw. The man's eyes glazed over just as Guy planted his right fist in his face. Milo staggered back, befuddled.

Two driving blows to the man's head knocked him onto his porch. Milo landed hard, his skull bouncing off the wall of the house. His hands fell uselessly to his sides, a groan escaping his lips.

Guy straddled him, taking a handful of his shirt, lifting him up, shaking him violently.

"Who'd you hire to kill Zack Lorring? How much did you pay him for killing a defenseless old man?"

But Milo only rolled his head from side to side, eyes dull and glasslike.

"I looked over the mines this morning, Milo. Your shaft had run dry. You had to have that other mine to survive. You had Zack killed to get that silver mine for yourself!"

"Go to blazes!" Milo snarled, coming out of his stupor. "You got no evidence against me."

"I'll get it," Guy vowed. "You're a big fish here in Crystal Creek, but this is only a small pond. I aim to drag you out into the sun and leave you to dry out, Gates. Before I'm finished with you, I'll know the truth about Zack Lorring's death."

Milo wiped at the blood that ran from his nose, sitting up under his own power. His eyes were full of raw hate. "You are a dead man, Kolter. When you've got a bullet in your gut and are dying in the dirt, I'll tell you who killed Zack. If I were you, I'd get on my horse and ride for my life!"

"Think I'll head over to the bakery instead and pick up something fresh and delicious for lunch. Can I pass along any messages for you?" Guy said.

"Just say your good-byes, Kolter. Your life is about to run out."

Guy walked up to the gate. Benny was just stopping his horse. It looked as if he'd been out all night.

"That was a pretty good shot last night," Guy told him matter-of-factly. "Dark as it was, I'm surprised that you got as close as you did."

Benny looked incredulous. "I don't know what you're talking about. I've been working all night."

"Your horse is showing red dirt from the hills, not the slag from the mine, Benny. Next time you ambush someone, take care not to bring home any sign of where you've been."

The man looked down at his horse's hooves. Then he frowned at Guy. He was scratching his head as Guy went up the street toward the bakery.

Nicole looked up from where she was cutting dough into squares. She didn't smile, but she didn't seem unhappy to see Guy in her shop.

"Don't tell me that you're hungry again?"

"I could get fat, being around a woman who cooks like you, Miss Monday. I've a craving for something sweet."

"I've just put some cinnamon rolls in the

oven. I had to let the dough rise most of the morning, but they should be done in a few minutes now."

"You must come in awfully early, trying to get all of your baking done."

"It's usually dark when I leave my house."

"Would you do me a small favor?" he said.

"What's that?"

"Don't leave your house until daylight for the next few days. I wouldn't want someone mistaking you for me."

That put a tight little frown on her face. "What have you been up to?"

"I started a few rocks rolling just now. If it turns into a rockslide, I wouldn't want you getting buried with me."

She moved over to look out her window, peering down at Milo's house. Her eyes naturally came back to look at Guy, finally spying the bloody knuckles of both his hands. Alarm sprang into her expression.

"Don't tell me you fought with Milo?"

"Wasn't much of a fight really. He kind of seemed to want to beat his face against my fists. I finally gave up. Tough man, your fiance."

"He isn't my fiance any longer."

That brought a smile to Guy's lips. "You don't say?"

She shot him a disturbed look, then turned back to her work. "It's what you wanted, wasn't it?"

"I think you're a person who'll be happier being in love than being able to roll in money, Miss Monday. You aren't the type of woman to marry just for material things."

"You know me so well, don't you? We've barely had a civil conversation, and you're already telling me what I want out of life."

"I'm a fully trained detective, Miss Monday. We detectives know many things that aren't shown on the surface. It's our job."

She sighed. "I guess I could have never gone through with a marriage."

"So why the engagement?"

She shrugged. "It just happened. Maybe I thought that I could learn to love him."

"You don't strike me as a woman with such poor judgment."

She changed the subject. "How many cinnamon rolls do you want?"

"Six ought to be enough for starters. I'll take them over to Pack's and get some coffee to go with them. I don't suppose you'd want to come along?"

"You've infuriated Milo enough for one day. I think it would be better if he didn't see us together, too. He as much as accused me of being . . . being taken with you."

Guy let a smile play along his lips. "I as much as told him the same thing. He was willing to blame me for the breakup of you two, and I find that rather flattering."

"That fattening food has gone to your head."

"The way to a man's heart is through his stomach—or hadn't you heard that saying?"

"I think it was a very fat man who made that quote."

"Nicole, would you like to know what I think of you?"

She ducked her head, a crimson flush climbing up her throat. "The cinnamon rolls are ready."

CHAPTER ELEVEN

Guy watched from the trees as Taco, Benny, and Flash took the two ore wagons up the road toward Silverton. Flash had a rifle across his lap, but there was little chance of any trouble on the ride to the smelter. The bandit only took the money. He evidently wasn't interested in the raw material, only the end result.

Guy figured that the three gunmen would likely return the day after tomorrow, or maybe a bit sooner. There were sturdy mule teams hitched to each wagon. They should make good time going and coming.

Even as he prepared to leave his observation point, he saw one of the Quinton boys sitting atop a knoll, also watching the wagons leave. Guy wondered again if the two of them weren't pulling these jobs. They'd told him that they were selling out come fall. Perhaps the sheep were only a cover. By fall, they would have every dime milked from Milo Gates.

The puzzle popped up again. Why only Milo Gates? There were other mines in the area, other payrolls going through from time to time. Even when robbing the stage, the Skull Mountain Bandit hadn't taken anything from the passengers and no other money from the strongbox. He'd only wanted the money going to Milo. There had to be a special vendetta between that bandit and Gates.

As had happened on other cases, Guy felt he had a partial answer, a clue, hiding in some corner of his mind. If only it would come to the surface! Oh, well, it would come in its own time.

As Guy rode back toward town, a lone rider appeared on the trail. He was dressed in a suit, with his warbag tied behind his saddle. From the way his saddlebags bulged, it appeared he was going on a long trip. For some reason, Guy wasn't surprised to find that it was Riley, the gambler. When the two riders drew close, Guy cut the other man off.

Riley stopped his horse and casually pulled a thin cigar from the inside of his coat and stuck it between his teeth.

He was lighting it as Guy asked, "You leaving the fair town of Crystal Creek?"

"I've starved here as long as I can, Kolter. With no payroll coming in, I've no miners to fleece. There's some diggings going on over at Del Norte and Monte Vista. That ought to be far enough away from Denver to keep my face unknown."

"Maybe you ought to go face the charges and get that warrant off your head."

"It'll drop in a couple more years and I won't have to worry about it anymore. As long as I can get my girl to take a chance with me, I'll risk any dodgers being tacked up. They'll hit some gold or silver farther west one of these days, and I'll move along."

"Great life you have to offer a woman, Riley. You're on the run, and you do nothing but hang around saloons and casinos night after night. That kind of life might be all right for a lone man, but you don't offer much of a future for a wife and kids."

"I'll maybe buy into my own place, once I collect a big enough stake."

"That Skull Mountain Bandit ought to have a sizable stake by this time. You figure he'll try and hit Milo's payroll again?"

"Be a fool to, what with Flash and Benny along. Those boys will be ready to shoot first and then worry about who they killed."

"I imagine you're right about that."

Riley grinned. "You're still wondering if I'm your man, aren't you?"

"A good many things could point a finger at you. If you pull out and the bandit disappears, it might even be proof enough for a man like Milo."

"I've no score to settle with Milo. If I robbed the stage the other night, I'd have taken everyone's money. Whoever this bandit is, he has something personal against Milo Gates."

"That could be a cover to throw any suspicion off the track."

"Well, I ain't saying that I'm your bandit, Kolter—nor will I claim I'm not. The question I'll put to you is, don't you think Milo deserves a little twist of the blade?"

"I've nothing against him personally," Guy said.

"That why you beat him senseless?"

"We were only discussing each other's faults. The conversation kind of became physical, but it didn't mean anything."

"Milo won't look at it that way. He's not known for his benevolent or forgiving manner. Once that money arrives to take the heat off him personally, he'll be figuring a way to get even with you."

"You think he's vindictive about that sort of thing?" Guy said.

"Well, Kolter, Milo never got anything dealing square. He came to this valley late, after silver had been discovered. Yet you notice who has the mines. He killed a family of homesteaders and ran off a couple of miners who valued their lives. The man plays his cards real dirty."

"How do you know that he killed anyone?"

"The blame fell on a Ute raiding party, but Ouray has kept his Indians out of trouble for a long time. Those people won't fight unless they feel threatened. Those homesteaders weren't threatening anyone, and they didn't even own decent horses. No Ute is going to get caught riding a nag. You know how they like to race. Why would they steal a broken-down animal and kill three people?"

"How do you know all of this?"

The gambler shrugged. "When men play cards, they often talk more freely than they should. I'm a good listener."

"If I was after the bandit, instead of looking for Zack Lorring's killer, I might put odds on you being my man, Riley."

The man's face lit up in a wide grin. "It'd take proof, Kolter, and the bandit never leaves any evidence lying about. If I was sticking around, I'd find it an interesting sight—you and the bandit working at a battle of wits."

Guy shot a curious look at the man's saddlebags. "I suppose if I asked to have a look in your gear, you'd take offense?"

Riley's hand was resting on the butt of his gun. "It'd have to be over my dead body, Kolter—if that's what you're asking."

"Like I said, I'm only after a murderer, not the bandit."

"Good luck pinning the rap where it belongs. Benny would be my guess, as Zack was shot in the back."

"I thought all of Milo's men were playing cards the night Zack was killed."

"Benny wasn't at the table much, and Taco was in and out. When you figure Ape only plays cards about once every blue moon, it was real peculiar seeing him play at all."

Kolter considered that. "So they were making a point of having an alibi."

"Sure looked that way to me. Benny is more of a back-shooter than a tough man in a fight. He'd be the likely choice for such a job."

"He tried to take me out not long ago." Guy rubbed the small hole in the pommel of his saddle. "At least, that's the man I guessed it to be."

"You pin him down and he'll crack, Kolter.

He's got the backbone of a snake."

"I'll remember that."

Riley lifted a hand. "I'll be seeing you, Detective. I've got an appointment to keep with a pretty girl."

"I probably shouldn't say this, but I wish you luck, Riley."

The gambler grinned again, then headed along the trail. He was moving at a leisurely pace, so there was little chance of his overtaking the ore wagons. If he had the stolen money with him, he could take his girl and start a fresh life some other place.

Guy considered his feelings toward the gambler. He knew the man was shrewd enough to be the bandit, but the vendetta against Milo was so personal. Could Riley have only been hitting on Milo to throw off any suspicion? Or was there a chance that the gambler actually had a reason for destroying Milo? Maybe he figured there was nothing wrong with robbing a murderer and thief.

Guy turned the thoughts over in his head, deciding to ride up and keep an eye on the Quinton boys. If someone did want to break Milo, then the sure-fire thing to do was stop this latest payroll from getting to the miners. It would be risky for a single bandit, but if he were twins . . .

Guy cut through the hills, hitting the trail below Nicole's cottage. He was about to reach a clearing, where he could see the woman's place, when he heard the distant echo of a single shot.

He stopped his horse, listening intently. All the birds were silent for a few seconds, then gradually picked up their usual chatter once more.

Guy turned his horse around, heading back down the hill. The shot had come from behind him, along the trail to Silverton.

Riley was already cold, his face buried in the grass, his gun still in its holster. He'd been shot in the back and probably hadn't even felt the pain.

Clothing, cards, his toilet kit—all were spread about on the ground. The saddlebags had been gone through, as had his blankets. Someone had thought he was carrying something valuable.

Guy tried to find some tracks, studying the ground. There were some bootprints. It appeared that someone else thought Riley was the bandit. If he had been the bandit, and if he'd been carrying the money he'd stolen, then it had changed hands. The gambler's luck had run out. His girl would wonder what had happened to him. They would have no life together now.

Guy picked up the things and then loaded the body onto Riley's horse. The trail of a single animal led back toward town, so the killer had thought to mix his tracks in with the regular traffic to Crystal Creek. It would work, for once lost among the other prints on the trail, there would be no way to pick up one set from the others.

Guy rode with suspicions running through his mind. He didn't doubt that Milo had had a hand in this. After all, that man was at the point where he'd suspect anyone of being the bandit. Riley's pulling out had put him in a bad light. He'd had the opportunity and was about the right size. He'd been in town since the holdups began, and he was up on the gossip and information about town from the miners. Riley could have easily gotten the schedule for the payrolls. And he came and went as he pleased.

Some things didn't fit so neatly, though. Why had he taken Benny's boots? Could it have been because he thought Benny had killed Zack and wanted to punish him a little? Was it a way of slowing down any pursuit that day?

And if Riley had a way of disappearing up in the rugged terrain, how did he get back to town without ever being seen?

Several people came out, seeing the body draped over the back of a horse. Milo appeared at the front of his house, but he didn't bother coming closer to have a look.

Pack was the man who told the carpenter a coffin was needed for Riley. The carpenter acted as undertaker in the town.

"Who did it?" Nicole asked. "Did you see who it was?"

"He'd already robbed and murdered Riley," Guy explained. "I was too far away when I heard the shot."

"What were you doing out in the hills?" Ape wanted to know, pushing in front of several miners.

"Snooping around, Mongold. Where were you about an hour ago?"

"He was here in town," Pack said.

"How about Milo?" Guy asked.

"What?" Ape cried. "What are you trying to say, Kolter?"

"That someone here ambushed and killed Riley. The tracks led back into town. He couldn't have arrived ten minutes ahead of me and Riley's body!"

"You've a big mouth, Kolter," Ape warned him vehemently. "Maybe I ought to shut it for you a second time!"

Guy faced the group. "Someone here must have seen whoever rode in a few minutes before I got here."

He looked around, but there were no talkers. If anyone had seen the ambusher return, he was keeping it quiet. Even Nicole only turned and went back into the bakery. She appeared pale and a bit shaken at seeing Riley's corpse.

"Maybe that Skull Mountain Bandit killed him," Ape finally said. "Ain't no one ever found out who he is."

"I believe that whoever killed Riley thought that Riley was the Skull Mountain Bandit."

That shut the man up. Ape evidently hadn't considered Riley in such a light.

As Riley's body was taken away, Guy went into Pack's cafe with him. The man poured them both a cup of coffee, then sat down at a table. Guy joined him, but he didn't drink any of the black liquid in front of him. Pack made an awful cup of coffee.

"You think Riley was the Skull Mountain Bandit?" Pack asked.

"I don't know for sure. He wouldn't admit

it, but he had good enough wits about him to have been the man. If he was pulling stakes, it wasn't smart of him to be seen doing it."

"I'll send a letter off to the county sheriff, less'n you want to handle it," the old-timer said.

"I don't live in your fair community, Pack. It'd be better for you to tend to it. I'll give you a deposition."

"A what?"

"A statement of what I saw and found."

"What about the case you're working on? Have you gotten any clues or evidence on Zack's killer?"

Guy said, "Benny is my prime suspect, but I'm sure it would have been on orders from Milo. I hope to pin Benny down, once he gets back from Silverton."

"I'd have bet money that Benny was the man on the trigger. He's too much of a coward to face anyone. Had it been Flash, he'd have shot Zack from the front. He thinks a lot of his prowess with a shooting iron."

"I can put some pressure on Benny, but it's going to be tough to pin a murder button on Milo. If I get close enough, the man will panic. That could get pretty rough."

"Could get you killed, sonny."

"I don't have any backup. With Milo's men

and guns behind him, it'll be tough to bring him to justice."

"You get in a fix, I'll be there with old Betsy! I done me some buffalo hunting for a spell once. I can shoot, if'n it comes to a war."

"I don't want a war. I just want to get the man who murdered Zack Lorring, and I'll also get the man who hired it done. Other than that, I have no connections with your fair town."

"The way you've been chasing after Nicole, it don't always look quite thataway." The old man grinned.

"You're a snoopy old cuss, aren't you?"

"That's one fine-looking woman, Kolter. She cooks up a storm, too. A man could sure do a lot worse than latching on to her."

"She might have something to say about that," Guy said.

"All you got to do is ask, son. She can't no more'n say no."

"I've got work to do. I still think there's some connection between the bandit and Zack's killer. A mystery like that gets under a man's skin. I'll worry about how to impress Nicole some other time."

"I hear you talking, son, but the words are a mite mixed up."

"See you later."

"Watch out for the arrows, Kolter." Pack laughed. "And I don't mean from the Utes. You watch for old Cupid. He'll be trying to get at you!"

CHAPTER TWELVE

Two days of watching the Quintons, and Guy
was no closer to any solid leads. The two men
appeared to be everything they claimed to be.
They did nothing but work sheep from daylight till dark.

As dark closed in on the second day, he decided to make his way down to the main trail.
He would keep an eye out for the return of
Flash and the other two men. They would have
had time to get their ore to the smelter and
pick up the money at the bank for Milo. If he'd
timed it right, they would either be through
that evening or the next morning. He would
get up the trail far enough to be out of sight,
yet able to follow the route they would take.

If Riley had been the bandit, his following would be for nothing. If someone tried to stop the three gunmen, Guy would be there to see what happened.

The boom of a gun told him that he'd been too slow to get down from his observation point. He tore through the brush, urging his horse to breakneck speed, bouncing down a deer trail. A few seconds later, the pop of handguns reached his ears. He swung wide of the main trail, staying back in the brush. If he guessed right, the bandit would head for Skull Mountain.

Out of the night came a phantom on horseback. A phantom dressed all in black.

"Hold it!" Guy called, pulling his gun, pushing his own horse right into the other's path.

The bandit veered off, shotgun coming around, twin barrels right in Guy's face. He drew his own weapon, but he knew he was going to be too slow.

The blast that would have taken Guy's head off never came. The black phantom's horse bolted into the trees, going at the pace of a runaway. Both rider and animal knew the trail.

Guy kicked his own horse into a run, right on the other's tail. He still had his gun out, but he hesitated at using it. He thought a minute, then holstered it.

By now the bandit's hoofbeats were growing fainter, fainter. Soon he was lost to Guy altogether.

Guy cursed himself, pulling his horse to a complete stop. He listened to the sounds of the night, but the rider was gone. He'd been right in the man's path, and still he'd lost him!

With his mount blowing hard under him, Guy wondered about his actions—not to mention the actions of the bandit. Either of them could have shot the other, but neither one pulled the trigger. He knew why he'd been slow to fire—he'd always been reluctant to kill another human being.

But what about the bandit? The barrels of the sawed-off shotgun had been right in his face. If the man had pulled the triggers, Guy would now be dead.

He had to consider the possibility that the bandit was not able to fire. He'd heard the loud boom of a scatter-gun. Perhaps the man hadn't bothered to reload his weapon. He might have fired both barrels during his holdup attempt.

That brought another question to mind. Did the bandit succeed in his attempt? Was he able to rob three gunmen—who were undoubtedly prepared for him?

The Skull Mountain terrain stopped Guy from pursuing the phantom further. He stopped at the base and took the animal trail that ran to the area where the Quintons kept their sheep. Then he kept riding. And soon he found himself looking at the lighted windows of Nicole Monday's cottage.

He reined over to the corral and looked for her horse. It was tethered a short distance away, picketed on a rope, able to eat the tall grass that was beyond the corral.

"I thought I heard a horse a minute ago." Nicole's voice came from the porch. "Where were you going?"

"It wasn't me," he replied, turning to find her standing with the lamplight behind her.

She automatically looked down the trail. "Then you're following someone?"

"The Skull Mountain Bandit."

She came forward, a full robe brushing the ground around her bare feet. Her hair was down, as if she were preparing to go to bed.

"I thought that...that Riley was the bandit," she said.

"Evidently not. You say you heard a horse just pass by?"

"Not five minutes ago. I thought it was just one of the Quintons."

He looked down from his horse, a stirring within him that had nothing to do with the bandit he was chasing.

"I'd better see if I can catch up with him. He's on a good horse. He ran away and left me on the trail up to Skull Mountain."

"Would you like to come in and rest for a few minutes? I can put some coffee on."

"I can't think of anything I'd like more, Miss Monday, but I better keep going. I might be able to pick out the bandit, if he goes straight to town. His horse will show a lather, and there are only so many suspects that I have to check out."

"Be careful," she said quietly.

"Good night, ma'am," he told her.

Then he was heading down the trail, riding for town. If he was lucky, he'd pick up the horse that had run for such a long distance. He'd try and find the owner from there.

As it turned out, there was a group of men already gathered in the street. When Guy rode into town, all eyes went to him.

"Where you been, Kolter?" Flash Tokat wanted to know.

"I followed the bandit along the base of Skull Mountain. He cut past Nicole Monday's cottage and came toward town."

"And how did you happen to be in the hills to start with?" Flash asked, his eyes narrow with suspicion.

"Just doing my job."

Milo came up to the crowd. His face was black with fury, his eyes smoldering like hot coals.

"And what's your job, Kolter? Who's paying you to chase after Nicole Monday?"

"My job, Milo, is to find out who killed Zack Lorring. You might have cause to worry about me doing just that."

"Don't you threaten me, you city slicker! How do we know that you ain't the bandit?" Milo asked.

"You were being robbed long before I got here."

"Yeah? Well, maybe you decided to take Riley's place! Maybe that's what the two of you were always putting your heads together about. Fact is, you probably killed him to cover your own tracks!"

Guy looked around the group. With the exception of Pack, they were all miners or worked for Milo. They were in an ugly mood.

"I can guess that you lost the payroll again," Guy said.

"Staring down the barrel of a 10-gauge shotgun, a man don't try his speed with a hand-gun," Flash replied.

"Any idea who it was?" Guy asked.

"He was about your size," Benny said. "Too dark to see his horse."

"Not so dark that you couldn't tell that it wasn't my roan," Guy shot back. "Think with your heads! Who's been missing for the past few hours? Who just arrived in town ahead of me?"

"Not a soul!" Milo shouted. "Since the boys come in, we've all been discussing this bandit business right here in the street. We'd have seen anyone coming up the road or trying to sneak into town."

Pack nodded. "That's a fact, son. Nary a soul has come into town since Flash, Benny, and Taco arrived."

"Where's Ape?"

"Right behind you, Kolter. I've been here the whole time."

"Is anyone missing from town?" Guy asked.

"Not a single man, Kolter," Milo growled.

"But the bandit was only five minutes ahead of me. Miss Monday heard him pass her place."

"Says you!" Flash snarled. "I say that you're the bandit we're looking for! You and Riley worked this up together. You killed him and brought his body into town. Now you've taken his place, robbing Milo's payrolls!"

"Don't be an idiot, Flash. I'm a detective, not a bandit!" Guy said.

But Flash quickly drew his gun.

At nearly the same time, Benny stepped up and took Guy's gun from the holster. He jammed it against Guy's ribs. "Let's walk over to the shed in back of Milo's house. It's nice and secure."

"Don't worry, Kolter," Milo sneered. "We won't hang you until you've had a fair trial."

"That's right." Flash grinned. "You'll get a square deal in the morning. We won't hang you until after you've had your say!"

"You men are crazy! This is Milo's way of covering up for the people he's killed. Don't tell me you're all such big fools!"

"I sent for this man," Pack said, stepping into the circle of men. "He's working for me. There ain't no way that he could be the bandit!"

"They're in it together!" Milo cried. "Pack is trying to break me and get back his mine! Sure! It all fits! These two jaspers are the ones who have been robbing me!"

"You're lying, Milo! You can't railroad me!" Guy said.

"Lock them both in the shed, boys!" Milo yelled. "Real tight!"

CHAPTER THIRTEEN

Nicole was fuming, storming about in front of the group of men. She purposely put herself between the crowd and Guy and Pack, defiantly poised against them.

"This is not a court of law. You have no right to try these men without a judge and jury! I won't stand by and let you make scapegoats out of these two men!"

"They'll have a chance to tell their side of it," Milo argued. "Why don't you go back to your bakery and bake something."

"Don't laugh at me, Milo Gates!" she hissed. "I'll have the sheriff down here and see you all behind bars! Don't you doubt my word for one minute about that!"

"These men have robbed me blind. I'm ruined, unless we can find out where they've hidden my money. Four thousand dollars is missing! Once a rope is around their necks— maybe then they'll talk!"

"No! I won't allow it!" Nicole snapped. "You men can't do this. Let a proper judge handle this affair!"

"The decision has been made, Nicole. You can remain during this hearing, but don't interfere again," Milo warned.

She stopped to look at Milo. His arms were folded to show his word was the law. The other men remained passive, as if the whole affair had nothing to do with them personally.

The trial was nothing more than a mockery. There was no evidence to support any claims, just idle talk. Riley was accused of being the original bandit. Guy was accused of killing him and taking his place.

It was said Pack had sold his mine to Milo, but wanted it back. It was also said Pack blamed Gates for the loss of his partner and had decided to bust Milo and his mine any way he could. Then it was said that Pack was behind both bandits—first Riley, then Guy.

"The sentence of this court is simple," Milo said at last. "If these two ruthless, murdering crooks wish to tell us where they've hidden my four thousand dollars, we'll give them a fifteen-minute head start out of the valley. If they get away, there'll be no further pursuit. That is giving them better odds than Riley got. If they don't want to cooperate, they'll both be hanged by the neck until they're dead—tomorrow morning!"

"You can't do that!" Nicole cried. "You haven't proven anything against either of them! You haven't given them a fair chance!"

"When they tell us where they've hidden their loot, we'll give them a fair chance, Miss Monday. This court is adjourned!"

Guy and Pack were roughly dragged back to the shed and shoved inside. Two guards were stationed out front. It was an adequate cell.

"Well, I got you into a real fine mess, Kolter. If'n you don't figure us a way out of it, I ain't going to feel obligated to pay you the other five hundred dollars I promised your agency."

"I don't blame you one bit."

Pack shook his head. "I can't understand the miners letting us be railroaded that way. They know I wouldn't get mixed up in nothing like robbing Milo."

"Everyone is looking for a scapegoat. Appears that we're the only ones available."

"Yeah, and once we've been hanged, Milo can take that four thousand dollars and start up my old mine good and proper. It's neat, all right. He blames all his loss on a bandit and uses his owed wages to better himself. The miners can't hold him responsible for the losses, and he only makes more money."

"You think that he's behind the Skull Mountain Bandit?" Guy asked.

"It don't read any other way, Kolter. It's got to be Milo."

"I don't know. We've accounted for all of his main men."

"Then one of the miners is in this with him. You can bet Milo ain't doing his own dirty work."

"There's still an outside chance that the Quintons are involved. I don't see how they could arrange it, but the trail always ends up in their country."

"They don't seem the type, but you could be right," Pack said.

"Come morning, it won't matter one way or the other. But maybe when they come to feed us, we'll get the chance to jump them."

"I wouldn't count on it."

"You have any better ideas?" Guy asked.

Pack looked around the shed. It was cluttered with junk. But nothing like a hammer or ax. There was nothing big enough to use to loosen the boards.

"We could try and hide under all this stuff, but I wouldn't count on them not finding us," Pack said hopelessly.

"Let's see if we can find something to use as a weapon. It would seem we're about down to our last resort."

Nicole threw her hands up into the air in frustration. She openly glared at the twins, but they remained unmoved.

"How can you just sit there and do nothing? Don't you give any consideration to your fellow man at all?" she cried.

"The man was doing a lot of snooping around here. He was asking to be put in his place," Leroy replied. "We only want to make sure you're all right. But the war going on here has nothing to do with us—and we want nothing to do with it. As we've always told you, we're willing to do anything for you that we can, but it don't mean we'll go get killed for you."

"A fine help you two are."

"Be reasonable, Nicole," Leroy said. "Milo has his gunmen sitting there, ready to kill anyone who tries to help those two. We didn't come into this part of the country to get ourselves killed."

"Why's this on your head anyway, Nicole?" Deroy asked. "Those two men are nothing to you. This isn't any of your affair."

"Not my affair!" she snapped. "You're the ones who are going to stand by while two innocent men are killed!"

"Seems they got themselves into the mess they're in. I reckon they'll have to get themselves out," Deroy said.

"And what if I happen to...to be in love with one of them?" She turned her face away from the twins, hiding the crimson flush that rose to her cheeks.

"You're joshing us, Nicole," Deroy said. "You don't mean that you're in love with that detective fella?"

"I—I don't really know. I've never been in love before. But I think it'll hurt me very deeply to see him killed."

Leroy was up on his feet and pacing now. "We never thought about anything like that, Nicole. That makes a difference."

She turned back toward them, looking at them pleadingly, then bursting into tears.

"I never seen you cry before, Nicole," Leroy said very gently. "You always seemed so strong."

"We'll help save your man, Nicole," Deroy volunteered. "What do you want us to do?"

She forced a halfhearted smile to her face, dabbing at the tears with a handkerchief. Guy

Kolter would have his chance. It was the least she could do for him and Pack—give them some kind of a chance.

Pack rubbed the bump on his forehead, while Guy nursed a cut lip and drew breaths that hurt his injured ribs. They had tried to escape at mealtime—and failed miserably.

"Yup, we sure took them by surprise," Pack grunted. "I thought that blasted Ape Mongold was going to kill you."

"You didn't fare much better against Taco and Benny," Guy said.

"Next time we'll do her the other way around. You take Taco and Benny, while I get killed by Ape," Pack said.

"What's worse, I'm getting hungry enough to start gnawing on my boots. We ruined any chance of getting even bread and water now."

"I ain't much caring if I get hanged on an empty stomach. I never was sentimental about that last-supper routine," Pack sighed.

"It's dark out," Guy said, looking through a crack in the wall. "Do you reckon this will be our last night on earth?"

"On it—yes. After this, we'll be under about six feet of it."

"Cheerful thought, Pack. You're a man who—"

"Fire!" someone called out in the distance.

Guy was on his feet at once, hurrying over to the door, trying to see what was going on.

Pack quickly rushed next to Guy, trying to peek through the cracks in the wall. "What's happening, Kolter? What's going on?"

"Don't move!" a voice softly commanded outside. "Drop those guns or die with them!"

Guy couldn't see who was speaking, for he was lost in the darkness, hidden deep in the shadows. Taco and Ape obeyed the man, throwing down their weapons.

"Now open the door," the voice commanded.

Guy waited until the bolted door was pushed open. Then he and Pack exited the small shack, still not knowing what was going on.

"Get their guns, Kolter," the mystery man directed. "Then you and Pack are on your own. Don't expect my help for a second chance."

Guy picked up one of the guns, and then the phantom was gone, lost to the darkness. There was no time to pursue their rescuer. He and Pack put Taco and Ape into the shed and locked them inside. Then they were making their way to the stable to grab their horses.

Once out of town, they stopped well off the main trail to discuss their next step.

"We need the law fast to back us up, Kolter," Pack said. "This whole thing has gotten out of hand."

"You're right about that, but how long will that take?" Guy asked.

"I'm for riding to Silverton and bringing back Larry Peters. He's a fair-minded sort of man. He'll see that no one gets lynched without a proper trial and jury."

"How long would that take you?" Guy asked.

"Maybe three days or more—if he's hard to locate. Otherwise, we might make it back in two."

"Then that's what you do, Pack. I'm going to see about getting a confession out of Benny. If we can break one of Milo's goons, it'll be him."

"That'd be a help, for Peters couldn't very well arrest us, while he was busy with that murder case on his hands."

Guy said, "I also hope to tie some loose ends together. Someone bailed us out tonight, and there can't be much doubt as to who was behind it."

"You figured out the Skull Mountain Bandit did it?"

"Some things are starting to fit together. If I get what I want out of Benny, I'll try and clear up the rest of this mystery later."

"Well, I'm all in favor of you doing that, son. Wish me luck on the ride. If Milo thinks I've gone for the sheriff, he might panic."

"You stay off the main trails coming back. We don't need another killing tagged to the Skull Mountain Bandit."

Pack grinned, "I didn't know you cared, son. You'll get me all choked up—worrying about my welfare."

"I'm only concerned about the five hundred you still owe my agency."

Pack laughed at that. "You ain't earned it yet." He thoughtfully narrowed his gaze. "And I ain't paying up if'n I'm dead. You best keep that in mind."

"Get a move on. With your head start, you shouldn't have to worry about any pursuit tonight."

"I'll be seeing you, Kolter. Try not to get yourself killed before the sheriff and me get back."

"So long, Pack."

Then the old man was reining his horse out toward the trail. He was quickly swallowed by the darkness, lost from sight.

Guy began edging his own horse back toward the town of Crystal Creek. It would be

difficult, but he had to keep tabs on Benny.
With the right approach, he would have Milo's
man squealing.

CHAPTER FOURTEEN

"We ain't going to find nothing out here in this dark," Ape called over to Taco. "Those two are miles away by this time."

"Boss said to look until we found them."

"Let him keep looking. I'm heading back. No need doing any more searching till it's light. Have to figure those two will be kicking up dust for a good many miles before they even look back. They'd be plumb crazy to ever come back to Crystal Creek."

"Which way did Benny go?" Taco asked.

"No telling. Let him worry about his own skin. Let's call it a night."

"I'm for that."

Guy listened to the two men, sitting his

144

horse back in the trees. The two hired guns would have been surprised if they'd known he was less than ten yards away. For he'd changed his mind about going into town when he saw Milo's men were searching for him in the countryside.

As Ape and Taco started back for town, Guy thought of Benny again. Benny was somewhere farther into the hills. He and Flash would be returning soon, all of them tired from the long chase into the night. There were only a certain number of routes that could be taken into town. The most logical was the path that ran down to the main trail. With luck, Benny would be riding from that direction soon.

Moving as silently as his horse could travel, Guy began to think of the best methods to handle Benny. Knowing the man's fears, he could use them against him. Once Benny was convinced that he was going to die, unless he started talking, it would probably be a real chore to shut him up.

Milo rubbed the sleep from his eyes. He glared at Flash, as if the man were responsible for all of his troubles.

"What are you talking about—the miners have quit?"

"Just what I said, Milo. Every last one of them is pulling up stakes. Most of the tents are already down. They're packing it in and moving on."

"They can't do that!"

"How do we stop them? They haven't been paid for a while, and everyone knows you had us bring every cent you could raise on our trip from Silverton."

"Surely, we can reason with some of them," Milo said.

"Nope. I spent an hour with them this morning. Every man jack of them is leaving."

Milo paced the room, his hands locked behind his back, wheels turning in his head. "But they know there's silver in Pack's mine. They know I'm good for the money."

"Remember you still owe Pack the final payment of five hundred dollars to get the deed to his mine. If you can't pay it within the thirty days, you lose the two thousand you gave him *and* the mine!"

"Then he'll soon own his mine again."

"That's the way the miners see it. If Pack was doing the hiring, I figure most of them would stay. As it is, they won't back your hand. You've got a cold deck."

Milo swore vehemently. "That blasted Skull Mountain Bandit has been out to ruin me—

and he's done it! How could one man do that to us?"

"Me and the boys will stick for another few days, boss, but I can't say for how long."

"You quitting me, too?"

"I haven't complained, boss. You know I wouldn't quit you unless I had to. But you're broke. You can't pay wages, and we can't eat promises."

"I've still got credit in town," Milo said.

"The Big Kitty Saloon is closing, and with the bakery burning down last night, this'll be a ghost town by the end of the week."

"I didn't know about the saloon," Milo said.

"He's tapped out. Our credit dried the owner right up. When you didn't pay the miners, they couldn't pay their bills. The whole town is flat busted."

"But we can get it back."

"How?" Flash asked.

"Everyone knows that Riley was the Skull Mountain Bandit. He must have hid his money someplace nearby."

"Yeah? Well, where do you think we should look?"

"How should I know? Kolter must have it. He and Riley probably struck up some kind of bargain."

"I don't know. We didn't find any of the

money on Riley. He had a few bucks, but it wasn't much of a stake for a gambler. He was as broke as the rest of us." Flash scratched his head thoughtfully and asked: "You think Riley would have trusted Kolter to handle the money end—providing they did strike some kind of bargain?"

"How do I know what the two of them did? You've got to find that Kolter and force the information out of him. If you and the boys want to get paid, we have to wring that money out of his hide!"

"What about the mine?" Flash asked.

"Pack will have a nasty accident, once we catch up to him. With him dead, no one will question my deed to his claim."

"I guess you're right. We can always find more miners to work for us."

"Right now, we need to locate Kolter. He's the key to this whole mess. Round up the boys, and we'll go have a look."

"Whatever you say, boss."

Benny whimpered like a child. With his hands tied behind him, he was helpless. He jerked his head from side to side, hoping to loosen his blindfold—with no luck.

"All right, Benny," Guy whispered ominously, disguising his voice, "it's time to meet the devil. If you believe in prayer, do your praying now!"

"No! Wait!" Benny cried. "Don't kill me!"

"You're a killer, Benny. You've killed people in this valley, and I imagine you've killed people before you came to Crystal Creek. It's time to pay for your crimes!"

"Look, Mr. Bandit, you got to give me a chance."

"Like the chance you gave Zack Lorring?" Guy demanded.

"How do you know about Zack?"

"And what was your role in killing those homesteaders—the ones Milo had to get rid of to stake his claim?"

"Listen, I can explain—"

"You even tried to kill that detective the other night. If you hadn't fired low, that would have been another death to add to your list!"

"Y—you know about that?"

"I know a lot about you, Benny. I know that you're about to die, unless . . ." He let the words hang.

"Unless?"

"If you'd care to tell me everything you know, I might just let you live. A judge would look

favorably on you, if you were to help put Milo
behind bars."

"I'd be killed if I even opened my mouth.
Flash would—"

Guy touched the blade of his knife against
Benny's neck, as if ready to cut his throat.

"Flash won't get the chance to do you in,
Benny. Say good-bye to the world!"

"No!" Benny wailed. "I'll talk! Don't kill me!
I'll tell you anything you want to know."

Guy released Benny, stepping back from the
cowering, sobbing back-shooter. He didn't like
to use such scare tactics, but he had no proof,
no evidence without a confession.

"You've got two minutes, Benny. If I think
you're lying, or if you try and cover up for your
own part in these killings, I'll just step over
and cut your throat. You understand me?"

Benny's head bobbed up and down. "I won't
lie to you, Mr. Bandit. I'll tell the truth!"

"Start with those homesteaders and staking
the claim."

"Their name was Roberts—a man, his wife,
and their son. Milo said to drive them out, but
they wouldn't go. Flash killed the woman, Milo
killed the boy, and I—I killed the man. But
he had a gun!" Benny added hurriedly. "We
didn't mean to kill them. It kind of got out of
hand."

"Go on," Guy ordered.

"There were a couple of miners who come snooping, but they were killed by Taco and Ape. I didn't have no part in that one."

"Continue."

Benny squirmed. "Everything was on Milo's orders. I only work for him. I only do what I'm paid to do."

"Like killing Zack Lorring?"

"Zack was a dangerous old coot. I couldn't take a chance with him," Benny said.

"How about Riley?"

"That was Flash. Milo thought Riley might be the Skull Mountain Bandit. He ordered Riley killed. I didn't have nothing to do with that."

"Why try and kill the detective?" Guy asked, still whispering.

"Milo was afraid he'd find something out. His snooping around was getting Milo worried. Mostly, I think Milo was getting even with him for taking away his girl."

"All right, Benny. I'm going to let you live. First off, I'm going to write down what you've told me. If you sign the paper, you'll stay alive to stand trial. If you refuse—" He laughed, a mocking sort of mirth.

"I'll sign! I'll sign!" Benny cried.

• • •

Guy left Benny strung up by his heels. There'd been some rope in the old cabin. With his feet off the floor, the gunman would be helpless. Guy could only hope that no one visited the abandoned miner's cabin—once used by Pack—before he returned. With luck, he might coax one of the Quinton boys into watching Benny until the sheriff arrived.

That idea flew off into the clouds, for the Quinton boys were gone. They hadn't waited around until the fall, after all. The herd of sheep had been moved out of the hills. From the tracks Guy could find, it appeared they'd left early that morning. The Quintons were most likely a good eight or ten miles out of the valley. They wouldn't be any help to him.

Guy turned automatically toward Nicole's cottage even though it was a dangerous place to visit. Milo might expect him to make contact with the girl, and someone might be watching the cottage.

Taking a roundabout route, Guy stopped his horse almost a mile from Nicole's place and went ahead on foot. It was slow, but he had to be sure he wasn't discovered.

He frequently stopped to take a careful look around. And his caution paid off when he spotted a big bay mare. It had been hidden in a hollow below the cottage, far enough away so that it wouldn't be exchanging whinnies with the big black that Nicole owned.

Lying on his stomach now, Guy used his ears as well as his eyes. Soon he heard a sort of thunk or plunk, like someone spitting out a wad of chewing tobacco. Then he heard the sound of footsteps from behind him. Guy clawed for his gun, turning over on his back. He spied Ape, only a few feet away. The big man's eyes were wide with surprise, but he was also grabbing for the gun on his hip.

Guy knew he had no choice but to fire.

The blast of his gun rocked the stillness of the woods. Ape was staggering from Guy's first bullet, but he still got his own gun free. Guy fired a second time, rocking the brute to his heels. Even so, Ape tried to line up his sights. The third bullet hit him high in the chest, knocking him backward. His own gun finally went off, but the bullet was lost in the sky.

Guy slowly stood up, his gun still trained on the mountain of a man lying on his back a few feet away. That had been close, very close.

Hurried steps came crashing through the brush. Guy spun around, prepared to meet another of Milo's men.

Nicole tried to stop so suddenly that she lost her balance. She stumbled forward—right into

Guy's arms. He caught her, keeping her from falling.

Instead of righting her, he lifted her into his arms, kissing her full on the mouth. He was rewarded at once, for her arms went around his neck. She unashamedly kissed him back, clinging to him as if her life depended on the security he offered.

"I—I heard the shots," she panted. "I—I was afraid that Ape had killed you."

"I expected someone to be watching your cottage."

"Are you all right? Is Pack all right?" she asked.

"He's on his way to bring the sheriff. I've got Benny locked up in Pack's old mining cabin. He signed a confession that'll put him and Milo behind bars."

"But Milo won't let you—"

"I'm going to see that Milo and the others don't ambush Pack and the sheriff. If the miners don't get in the way, I might figure out a way to confine the three men who'll be tried for murder."

"Benny confessed everything?" Nicole asked.

"Names, dates, the works. Your old boyfriend is going to hang."

She colored noticeably. "He was never my boyfriend. I was—"

He kissed her, preventing her from saying anything more. He enjoyed holding her, but he had to put her down. There was a dead man to tend to. There were things that couldn't wait.

"I've got to take Ape into town. I'll be back for you when this is over."

"There are no miners left to contend with, Guy. When I went in and found that my bakery was burned to the ground last night, I heard a number of them say they were leaving."

"Some coincidence, your bakery burning down, while the bandit turned us loose."

"I heard about that," she said.

"I imagine you did."

"What do you mean by that?"

He grinned. "We'll discuss it when I return. Once I earn my wages, I'll be due a couple weeks' vacation. Might even be time to find a nice house and take a honeymoon."

Nicole smiled demurely. "Are you asking me to marry you?"

"Be pretty silly—honeymooning all by my lonesome."

"Mrs. Guy Kolter. I guess I could live with that."

"It's a date then. I'll just tidy up some first, before the sheriff arrives. Got to have everything in a neat little package so we can get this over with."

"Be careful," she said.

"Don't worry about that. I've got too much to live for to take any unnecessary chances."

Then Guy got to work. He had to take Ape into town and find a way to disarm and lock up Taco, Flash, and Milo. It would not be easy.

CHAPTER FIFTEEN

It was dark before Guy managed to unload
Ape at the carpenter's place. He found that
the carpenter was one of the very few people
left in town. And the man was glad to share
his supper with Guy. It wasn't much, but it
sure was better than nothing.

Slipping back out of town the way he'd entered, Guy found a spot to conceal his horse.
Then, heading toward town once more—and
Milo's house—he wondered if anyone had
found Benny yet. It really didn't matter, for
he had the man's signed confession. He could
always pick Benny up later.

A light was on in the Gates house. After
watching for a time, Guy decided to go have

a look inside. His timing was almost disastrous, for Taco rode up just as Guy was at a rear corner of the house.

Milo came out the front door to greet the gunman. Guy couldn't see him, but he could tell it was the boss himself. He strained his ears to hear what was being said.

"Ape wasn't there?" Milo was saying.

"No horse, no Ape—nothing out there."

"What about Nicole Monday?" Milo asked.

"She was gone, too. Looks to have taken her big black and ridden him off."

"I don't get it. Where could Ape be at?"

"If the girl left the house, he might have followed after her."

"Those weren't my orders," Milo said.

"Well, I found where he'd been sitting. His chewing habit told me that. I saw where he'd been hiding and spitting his chaw. There was a bit of blood on the ground."

"His?"

"Don't know. That's all I found," Taco said.

"Things are getting awfully queer around this place. First Benny disappears, and now Ape has vanished."

"Must be the work of that detective fellow."

"It was that miserable bandit who turned him and Pack loose. I can't believe our bandit is still running loose," Milo grunted.

"Could have been anyone dressed up in black, boss. Nobody knows who he is, so everyone in the country could put on a black thing over his face and say he's the Skull Mountain Bandit."

"Flash will deal with him if he tries to prevent Flash from ambushing the lawman from Silverton."

"You think someone's bringing the sheriff here?" Taco asked.

Milo said, "Maybe Pack. That detective will want law on his side before he tries anything drastic. Our only chance is to catch Kolter and find out what he did with the money."

"It might not be Kolter. That could have been the real bandit who let him and Pack go. He looked about the same to me."

"No one else is left!"

"Could have been one of the miners."

"Flash and I accounted for every man after each holdup," Milo said. "Riley was the bandit. I'm for thinking Kolter took his place. The man who rescued him was probably his backup man from Denver. Detectives often work in teams. He has a man out there we haven't seen yet."

"What do you want me to do?" Taco asked.

"Get some chow and some rest. If Ape doesn't show by morning, we'll go out and round up Kolter."

"All right, boss. I'll stick with you another day, but if that sheriff shows up, I'm setting fire to my horse's tail."

Guy quietly padded back into the darkness. He went to his horse and opened his saddlebags. After digging out two pairs of handcuffs, he returned to watching Taco.

The man took his horse to the livery stable and spent a few minutes tending to the animal. Then he headed down the street, going to look for someplace to eat. Guy remained out of sight, following about two buildings behind him. When he saw the carpenter come forward and speak to Taco, he knew word was being given about Ape's fate.

Guy ran down an alley between two buildings and hurried back in the direction of Milo's house to get to a point—up another alley— where he could intercept Taco. He found a sturdy two-by-four on the ground and decided that it would be an equalizer to counter the hardness of Taco's head.

The gunman came up the path at a jog, hurrying to tell Milo what he'd learned. As he came even with the alley, Guy darted out, swinging the thick piece of wood at its target.

The man's body kept traveling, even after his head and shoulders had suddenly come to a stop. As a result, Taco's feet ran right out from under him. He hit the ground flat on his back, arms flung uselessly at his side.

Guy dragged the man quickly out of sight, hauling him down the alley. Once he reached the trees, he found one small enough so that he could put the man's back to it and handcuff him around it. With his back to the tree, Taco wouldn't be able to even work against the gag Guy had placed in his mouth.

He shook the gunman awake, but Taco was still dazed. Guy decided the man wouldn't be doing much of anything the rest of the night. Upon examining the big lump on the man's forehead, he had to wonder that Taco was even able to open his eyes.

"You really should be more careful about where you're going, Taco. A man could get hurt, running around in the dark and bumping into things."

The man only closed his eyes, unconscious once more. He wouldn't be any trouble for a time. Guy could concentrate on Milo, then go after Flash. Flash Tokat was Guy's big worry. He feared Milo's top man might kill Pack and the sheriff. He had to prevent that, even if it meant killing Flash. But first he must deal with Milo.

Guy turned back toward Milo's house. He would sneak up to the windows and locate the man responsible for the murder of the Roberts family, Zack, a couple of miners, and the gambler, Riley. Milo Gates was a man that Guy might even enjoy seeing at the end of a rope. He'd taken and killed indiscriminately and grown fat on his profits. If not for the Skull Mountain Bandit, he would have gotten completely away with it, too.

Guy was too late, reaching the house, for Milo had already left. Pausing in the dark, Guy wondered what had taken place. There was a good chance that the carpenter had come over and told Milo about Ape. If so, he had surely mentioned Guy, too.

Had Milo panicked? Would he simply pack up and run? That didn't seem likely. He was more of a fighter than that. He would seek safety in numbers, and with Taco and Benny temporarily out of action, that left only Flash. Milo was probably with him right now.

There was no chance for Pack to return until late the next day—at the very soonest—so he put off looking for Milo. He would deal with both Flash and Milo after he'd had a few hours' sleep. There wasn't a safe place in town, and he had to check on Benny and fix him something to eat. After all, the man was a prisoner. He was rotten, no good, a back-shooter, but he was in Guy's custody.

He would take Taco out to the miner's cabin and see if he could figure a way to confine the two of them. If he shackled them together, they wouldn't be able to get very far.

Deciding on that course of action, Guy worked his way down to the livery stable. Milo's horse and tack were gone. Yes, he was probably with his number-one gun, Flash Tokat. Tomorrow was sure to be rough.

Guy took Taco's horse and made his exit carefully. Once he handcuffed the Mexican to his saddle, he was moving into the night, following the trail he'd come to know. It was slow, with a dark path under a moonless sky.

By the time he reached the miner's cabin, he guessed it to be around midnight. To his surprise, there was a horse staked out in front of the place—Nicole's horse!

She came out to meet him with a pistol in her hands. He had to smile, pulling up where she could see him and Taco.

"I heard mention that you weren't at your

cottage, Nicole. It didn't occur to me that you'd have come here."

"You couldn't very well move about and keep an eye on Benny. He was practically loose when I arrived. I've kept my gun on him for so long that my arms are stiff."

Guy took Taco inside and then shackled the two men together — back to back around a pot-bellied stove.

Nicole fixed a plate of beans for the prisoners, and then a little something for Guy. He hadn't digested the meal he'd had earlier, but he felt that he would need the strength.

"I want you to get some sleep," Nicole told him once he'd finished eating. "I'll keep an eye out for any riders."

"A man could get used to having someone around like you," he told her.

"When this is over, perhaps you'll get a chance to find that out for certain."

"I'll remember that," he said.

"Now get some sleep. You've got to keep Milo and Flash from ambushing Pack and the sheriff tomorrow. That won't be easy."

Guy settled down on the only cot. By the time his head hit the hard mattress, he was already asleep.

CHAPTER SIXTEEN

Milo scoured the area, but Flash was not watching the trail. In fact, the man was nowhere to be found. Things were getting out of hand. First Benny had up and disappeared, and Taco had vanished, and then Ape was killed out at Nicole's place. Warned by the carpenter that the detective was in town, Milo had to figure he'd taken care of Taco. Now Flash was not at his appointed place.

Turning his horse around, Milo put him on the trail toward town. He knew that Kolter wouldn't hang around town too long. He didn't know what the man was up to, but it was unlikely that he could keep track of every man on Milo's payroll. If he was human, he would have to rest. That meant he would hole up somewhere for the night. Milo needed to find Flash and put some kind of plan into action. First off, he needed to know why Flash wasn't at his post.

He decided to see if Flash was in his room above the saloon. Outside the door, Milo drew his gun, just as a precaution. Then he entered Flash's room. Instead of being asleep, Flash was sitting on his cot—with a pile of money on either side of him!

"Hold it!" Milo roared. "Don't you move a muscle, Flash!"

The man froze, dropping a handful of bills. He looked at the gun in Milo's hand and shook his head.

"Whoa, now, Milo. Don't you be thinking what I think you're thinking. This money was stashed here, but I didn't bring it into the room. Someone left it here!"

"How much is there, Flash—maybe four thousand dollars?" Milo sneered, his eyes narrowed with suspicion.

Flash licked his lips, his eyes darting nervously at the gun in Milo's hand. He shifted his weight carefully, but kept his hands away from his gun.

"It's the payrolls. The bandit planted them here."

"Sure. Now maybe you'll tell me who the bandit is, Flash—or is it you?"

"Me?" Flash was incredulous. "How could it have been me? I was on the wagon that was robbed!"

"Only you got a look at the bandit. His gun-blast was supposed to keep the heads down of the men behind you. Maybe I guessed wrong about Kolter. It's been you all along, you and Riley. Then you double-crossed Riley and took the money all for yourself."

"That's crazy, Milo. I'm not the Skull Mountain Bandit!"

"Then explain those clothes!" Milo pointed at a pile of black garments strewn on the floor next to the cot.

Flash reacted at once. When Milo's gun swung toward the black clothing, he was drawing his own gun. He was fast—incredibly fast.

Milo hadn't been ready to kill. He was surprised that Flash would draw against him. It was all the edge the gunman needed. The blast from his deadly .44 was accurate and fatal.

Hit hard in the chest, Milo staggered back toward the door. He still had the gun in his hand, but he couldn't turn it on Flash. When a second bullet jolted him, he found himself sitting on the floor.

Flash looked at him with disdain, walking over and holstering his gun with a cynical grunt.

"You're a fool, Milo. You've always been one, and now you're dying like one. I'd have shared this loot with you, but you pointed your gun at me. No one points his gun at Flash Tokat— no one!"

The words were too far away for Milo to hear. Even the sight of Flash faded until he was only a blur. All Milo knew was pain and a growing dizziness, a coming blackness.

Flash laughed at him. "You're a big man, Milo, a big fool. I'm going to take this money and live like a king. First off, I'm going to kill that pesky detective. Because I figure that he's the bandit. Then it'll be the sweet life for me." He tipped his head toward the cot, still covered with piles of money. "Thanks for the stake, Milo. Whenever I spend it, I'll be thinking of you!"

Guy went into town the next morning. He had to be certain that Milo wasn't gathering more men or making a run for another state. What he found was the carpenter and the few men left in Crystal Creek laying out the body of Milo Gates.

"It makes sense," someone was saying. "Flash was the Skull Mountain Bandit all along. He was probably working with Riley."

"Why did he let me and Pack go?" Guy asked.

"Guess he wanted some confusion," a thin man said.

"Probably figured to blame Milo's death on you or Pack," said another. "Might have worked if I hadn't heard the two shots last night. I got up to Flash's room first and found the black outfit. Flash was beating his horse out of town not two minutes later."

"Yeah, I seen him come out of the building," the thin man said. "Wasn't no one else around. Flash is the man, all right."

"Anyone see which direction he took?" Guy asked.

"He was headed over the hills. No telling where he'd go, but you can bet it won't be Silverton."

Guy mounted his roan and set out in the direction Flash had taken. He didn't travel far before he picked up the tracks of a single horse. He was a good four hours behind the man, but the mountains were rugged for the first fifty miles. Flash wouldn't make much time, and Guy might cut the distance with a lucky break. He could hope Flash would be tired, leaving in the middle of the night. It was certain that the man's horse would be worn out by tonight. If he pushed his own mount, he might make up the necessary miles by dark.

Up into the higher terrain he climbed, among the spruce and pine. The air was crisp, clouds rolling in from New Mexico and threatening to build into a major storm.

Pushing his horse for more speed, guy soon found that they were on a fairly well-used trail. He didn't know where it led, but it had been ridden by horses often enough to be very distinct. If not for the constant climbing, it wouldn't have been a hard trail to follow.

Around midday Guy was walking on foot, allowing his horse to regain its wind. He walked as rapidly as he could, gasping for air. He definitely felt he had gained on Flash. Now he was only two hours behind his prey.

Mounted once more, Guy kept up the torrid pace. If he didn't catch up to Flash that night, he might lose him for good. The man would be tired. He would have to stop early. That was what Guy told himself, keeping his horse on the move.

It was during the long hours of pursuit that Guy's thoughts returned to his recent battle with Ape. He had reacted quickly, firing without hesitation. But then he'd known Ape was a deadly killer. And maybe he'd learned something from his partner's death several months ago. All the same, Guy hoped he never shot a man unless it was absolutely necessary.

The sun sank low on the horizon, but Guy kept his horse moving. He dug out some jerky and ate in the saddle, his eyes always on the trail ahead, always wary. He wouldn't underestimate a man like Flash.

With his rifle out, the butt against his hip, fingers laced above the trigger guard, Guy kept out a sharp eye for ambush. If Flash decided to stop and check his back trail, he would most certainly fire on a lone horseman.

The lead he had was one of the things that might cause Flash to be careless. He might even think that no one would come after him. Not for a long while. After all, with Milo dead, who was going to hunt him down?

Darkness set in, with no moon to light the way. Fortunately, the path was wide and deep. Guy continued to move along it, leading his horse most of the time. He grew more cautious as the night wore on, stopping, listening, even trying to pick up any scent in the air.

Walking softly, eyes probing the dark, Guy suddenly stopped. There was a smell of smoke on the evening breeze. Flash was so confident there would be no one following that he'd built a fire!

Guy tied up his horse and proceeded carefully through the brush, soundlessly, painstakingly. He kept his rifle at the ready.

The fire was down in a hollow, surrounded by brush and some old dead pine. The flames were very low. And a coffeepot sat on a rock next to the fire. Flash was partially visible, but there were small trees and some brush between Guy and his target. He had to get closer. A night owl hooted, and Guy took a deep breath and set his teeth.

He crouched down and moved a couple of steps.

A blast from Flash's gun shattered the silence. Guy dove for cover, hearing the slug thud into a nearby tree. He crawled behind a dead log and risked a peek over the top. Flash was not in sight.

"Give it up, Tokat!" he called. "I've got a posse with me. You're surrounded!"

"You're lying through your teeth, Kolter," Flash retorted. "You're the only man fool enough to come after me."

"I aim to take you in, Flash. You, Taco, and Benny will have your say in court."

"No deal, Kolter. I'll just have to kill you instead."

"I don't kill easy, Flash. You can ask Ape about that."

"Ape was no gunman, Kolter."

"I don't want to have to kill you. Make this easy on yourself." As Guy spoke, he crawled a few feet, trying to pinpoint the location of Flash's voice. He needed to locate the man before any shooting started.

"Maybe we could strike some kind of bargain, Kolter. What would you say to taking a thousand dollars and riding away?"

"That's a lot of money. You sure you want to waste it?"

"I don't like the idea of killing you," Flash said.

"Is that why you left such a clear trail?"

Flash laughed. "Noticed that, did you?"

"A six-year-old could have followed you. You must have expected me to come."

"I knew you'd follow, Kolter. You had to be the bandit who left me all that money. I intended to kill you all along. As a matter of fact, I was going to sit and wait for you tomorrow. You made good time getting this far."

"How were you going to do it, Flash—in the back?"

"Does it matter?"

Guy said, "Just curious if you were a real man or not. Looks like you and Benny were cut from the same bolt of cloth. You're both back-shooters!"

"You talk real big, Kolter. Real big."

Guy searched the darkness, but he couldn't find Flash. The man was only a voice in the night. And he was quick enough with a gun to brag about how good he was. Guy could only wonder if the man was really that good. If so, was Flash faster and more accurate than he? Again that night owl hooted in the darkness. Perhaps the bird was wondering about the single shot that had been fired.

"What do you say, Kolter? Cat got your tongue?"

"I'm listening, Tokat. What do you suggest now?"

"We could settle this like men. Are you game for something that takes real guts?"

"Just you and I, standing face to face—is that it?" Guy asked.

"You got it."

Guy again took a deep breath. His heart was thundering. His every nerve was alert.

"What's your idea, Tokat?"

"You've heard that night owl?"

"I've got ears," Guy said.

"We step out into the fire's light, guns in our holsters. When that fellow sings out again, we draw."

"You must think you're pretty good, Flash."

"I am, Kolter. What about you?"

"Passable."

"So what do you say?" Flash asked.

Guy knew that Flash was confident of being the fastest of the two. But maybe he was better than Flash anticipated. Also, the man must be very tired by now. His reaction time would be a mite slower than usual. Maybe.

"All right, Flash. I'll step into the light as I see you appear. We both holster our guns slowly, then move in closer."

Guy raised himself up slowly, still holding the rifle. Even as he stared across the campsite, he saw Flash edging toward the light. The man's pistol was in his hand, but he didn't have it pointed toward Guy.

Guy carefully put down his rifle. Then he lifted his handgun out of the holster, matching the very move that Flash was making.

They approached the fire, each man holstering his pistol carefully. Eyes were wary, hands poised over the guns. They froze in position, each waiting for the sound that would mean the possible death of them both. Neither of them spoke, for no words could stop them now. Nerves were sharp, every sense alert, hearts pumping.

The quiet was intense. It seemed that the owl would never hoot again, that the two of them would stand poised against one another until daylight. Then the owl cried again.

Guy's hand shot to his gun, jerking it free. Flash was matching his motion. They fired almost together, their weapons spitting fire and death.

Guy's left side was hit. Spinning around, he fell down. But he rose to his elbows, trying to get his gun pointed for a second shot. He saw Flash aiming his gun. He would be too slow to return Flash's fire. He was going to die!

CHAPTER SEVENTEEN

A gun boomed in the darkness. Guy waited for the impact, knowing he was as good as dead.

But it was Flash who was knocked down flat, arms out to his sides. He was dead before he'd hit the ground.

Guy put a hand to the pain just above his left hip. He pressed his fingers tightly against the wound, stopping the bleeding. Then he tried to find the man who had saved his life.

Nicole Monday came out of the darkness. She had a short-barreled shotgun in her shaking hands. Her eyes were transfixed on the body of the man she'd just killed. She stopped after a couple of steps and looked down at her gun.

"I—I couldn't let him kill you," she said.

"He was faster than me. I hurried my shot and missed him. He had me cold, Nicole. You saved my life."

She threw the shotgun into the brush and ran over to him. After a glance to see that Guy wasn't seriously hurt, she came into his arms.

"I was so afraid...I couldn't stand the thought of waiting. I had to...had to follow after you."

"Lucky that you did. Our kids would have been real unhappy if you'd have let that man kill me."

"Let's bandage that wound. It looks clean, but we'd better treat it at once."

"Good idea. Then you can round up Flash's horse. We'll stake out the animals for the night and start back in the morning."

An hour later, Guy was lying on a blanket. He sipped at some coffee, but Flash didn't make any better cup of mud than Pack did.

Nicole sat down next to him, their blankets close to the fire. She was quiet for a while but finally spoke up. "I guess it's all over now. Taco and Benny will stand trial for murder and be sentenced. With Milo dead, Pack will get his mine back."

"And the Skull Mountain Bandit?" Guy

asked, nodding toward Flash's saddlebags, where they'd found the money.

"Gone forever."

"Want to tell me about it?"

"About what?" she said.

He looked into that innocent face, the eyes dark and expressive. She played her role well.

"I know that you're the Skull Mountain Bandit, Nicole. I have for some time."

"I don't know what you mean! Riley and Flash were working that bandit routine!"

"Want me to go dig your shotgun out of the brush?"

"What for?"

"It would be a 10-gauge Meteor. That's what Benny said it was when I met you that first day."

She shook her head, as if totally shocked by his accusation, but he went on.

"That bruise you gave yourself on the head was a neat trick. You stopped me from searching the hills and won my sympathy all at the same time."

"You really think I'm the bandit?" she asked.

"I don't doubt it at all," he replied. "That night I followed him to your cottage you had your horse picketed off the main trail. I didn't think much about it, until I got to town and found out that no one had entered ahead of me. You always put your horse in the corral before that."

"You convict me on that flimsy evidence?"

"When we met on horseback, you could have shot me—you didn't. In fact, you never fired to kill anyone until tonight. You got close to Milo to find out when and where his money was coming in and you broke him. Since Flash ended up with the money, you weren't doing it to get rich. I figure that it was for revenge."

"Revenge?" she said.

"Yes, Miss Nicole Roberts—revenge."

Nicole sighed, lowering her head. "Why didn't you say something?"

"I wasn't a hundred percent sure until you had the one Quinton boy turn us loose. When I saw him run off, I knew then that you were the bandit."

"How?"

"A man fills out an outfit a little differently than a woman—even from the back. I'd seen you ride a horse and walk away from Benny. I was able to tell the difference."

"I see why you're a detective. What else do you know?"

"You said you'd been sent away to take care of your grandmother. I figure that Milo must have arrived shortly thereafter and killed your brother and parents."

"I was taken in by the Quintons," Nicole admitted. "They were good to me. I lied about the wicked stepmother. Anyhow, they weren't willing to let me strike out on my own, so the twins came here with a herd of sheep. They were to see that nothing happened to me."

"And you dealt out your own punishment to Milo?"

"He killed my parents and brother. I was determined to gather proof against him. I might have, if you hadn't come to the valley and stirred everything up."

"You were already holding up his men before I came to Crystal Creek," Guy reminded her.

"I had to slow him down. He was going to take over the entire valley. It was only my influence that made him try and buy Pack out. I know he had intended to kill both Zack and Pack."

"And you stole Benny's boots because a woman's shoe isn't really made for riding?"

"Not astraddle," she admitted. "Of course, I'd have to get away from here before I could risk wearing them."

Guy let out a sigh. "My betrothed, the Skull

Mountain Bandit. What am I to tell our children about that?"

"More importantly, what will you tell the sheriff about that?"

"What's to tell? Flash and Riley were masquerading as the Skull Mountain Bandit—just ask anyone left in Crystal Creek."

Nicole looked closely at him. "Then... then you aren't going to turn me over to the arms of the law?"

"He'd want to keep you for himself," Guy replied. "The only arms you're going to be in are mine."

"Oh, Guy!" Nicole cried, throwing her arms around his neck and kissing him.

He flinched from the pain that shot through his injured side, but it felt good just the same. With Nicole in his arms, he figured he'd always feel good.